THE First PLAY

KATY ARCHER

Katy ♡ xoxo Archer

THE FIRST PLAY
Nolan U Football #0.5

© Copyright 2025 Katy Archer
www.katyarcher.com

Cover Design © Designed with Grace
www.designedwgrace.com

ISBN: 978-1-991138-70-5 (Kindle ebook)
ISBN: 978-1-991138-72-9 (paperback)

Archer Street Romance
www.katyarcher.com

CHAPTER 1
ZANDER

I am so wrecked.

My muscles curse me out as I roll over in bed with a groan.

Yesterday's away game was brutal. And it didn't help that I got sacked in the first quarter. The crowd had a field day, screaming in triumph as I lay crumpled under the big-ass defensive end who got through our offensive line like they were welcoming him in for a fucking party. For a guy that huge, he was a stealth ninja. I didn't even see him coming. But I felt every ounce of him.

The tackle knocked the air right out of me, but I played the rest of the game, because that's what you fucking do when you're a Nolan U Cougar. Coach asked me if I needed a minute, but hell no. I was fired up and ready to annihilate the Fort Collins team.

Tyrell was so pissed I got sacked, he gave his guys a rocket up the ass, and for the rest of the game, I was protected at every turn. It was like playing behind a wall of titanium warriors, and even though Fort Collins made us work for it, we won.

So, despite the aching muscles, a smile stretches over my face.

Until it drops away when I think about how much studying I have ahead of me today. It's Sunday, which means no games, no practices, and a shit ton of schoolwork to catch up on.

"Fuck." I scrub a hand down my face and force myself out of bed. It's already eleven thirty, and I can hear guys up and about downstairs. I wonder if they're mainlining coffee the way I need to right now.

I should have gone to bed as soon as we got home last night, but Grady started up the Xbox, and you don't just turn your back on a *Call of Duty* invite. We needed to unwind anyway, and Coach had warned us about not getting off the bus and going out to party.

"You need to let your body replenish. Take some downtime, rest up, and get yourself ready for a new week on Monday. I expect you all to be in class, on time, your work up-to-date." He clapped his hands while we all stifled groans. He was about the only college coach in the country who went on about classes and shit. He wants us to do well in every area of our lives. We're constantly getting lectures and pep talks about our physical, mental, and spiritual well-being, and it's not all to do with football. Coach Jones wants us to be more than just athletes. "I'm training you for life, remember. It's more than just a game." He pointed at us like he always does, his finger wagging in the air like a drumstick. "And I'll see you at practice on Monday afternoon."

Carson rolled his eyes, growling in his throat. I don't know why. He was going to ignore Coach Jones anyway. The guy never followed the rules, much to my annoyance. I was constantly having to cover for him when all I wanted to do was smack him up the side of the head and tell him to watch himself. He's the best wide receiver I've ever worked with, and if he'd stop fucking up so much off the field, I'd be a happy man. I just don't want to see him get benched... or end up dead because of some drunken, reckless stunt he pulled at a party.

Stretching tall, I glance at my desk and the stack of books beside my laptop. I have so much work to do, but I can't think about that right now.

"Coffee," I croak, pulling on a pair of sweats and a crumpled T-shirt.

Clomping down the stairs, I peek my head into the living room and spot Carson slumped on the couch. He's wearing shades and nursing a coffee mug. He must have gone out for a hookup after we finished *Call of Duty*. Idiot. I shake my head and raise my chin at Wily, who's grinning at me like he woke up on a ray of sunshine and danced through white puffy clouds on his way downstairs. His laptop is on his knees, and he's obviously trying to study while watching *The Punisher* with Carson. No wonder the guy is always on the edge of flunking out. He hates schoolwork with a passion, but Coach is a hardass. He *will* bench our asses if our schoolwork isn't up to scratch. I'm sure the guy has gotten into plenty of arguments with the AD over it, but he refuses to let up.

"They're not just players, dammit!" I heard him yell once. *"We need to give these guys a chance at real life too!"*

A grunt comes from the TV, and I spot Frank Castle punching some asshole in the face before I glance back to Wily.

"Sup, Cap?" I don't know how the fuck he does it, but the guy is always cheerful... sometimes to the point of being fucking annoying. His big dopey smile can win over anybody, though.

"Nothin' much. Need me some coffee." I stroll into the kitchen and find Grady frying up a feast.

I sniff the air, my stomach rumbling. "Can I have in on that?"

"Make your own fucking breakfast." He grins at me.

I laugh and lightly punch his shoulder before pulling out the bacon and slapping it down beside him. "Thanks, bro."

"How many slices?"

"Gimme five with two eggs and I'll make the toast."

"Any hash browns?"

"Nah." I untie the bread bag and start manning the toaster while also pouring myself a much-needed coffee.

I sip that hot brew and let out a satisfied sigh.

"Yeah, I feel ya, man. Those fuckers were like a horde of zombies yesterday," he mutters. "I only got tackled once, but it was like being hit by a slab of concrete."

"Tell me about it," I mumble, turning back to the toaster. "Hey, do you know where Carson went last night?"

"Not sure." Grady shrugged. "I went to bed and just hoped like hell we wouldn't get some phone call at four in the morning telling us to come to the hospital."

"What the fuck are we gonna do with him?" I huff. "I

thought he'd gotten his shit together after nearly getting kicked off the team last year."

"Yeah, he definitely improved there for a while. But then summer happened."

I clench my jaw.

"But he played like a demon yesterday, man. At least he's lightning on the field."

"Yeah." Refilling my mug, I pull out the plates and butter the toast before Grady loads us up.

We eat in silence, Grady scrolling through TikTok videos and smiling at clips of... probably morons in cars or dogs acting crazy. The guy loves to watch mindless shit.

Meanwhile, my mind is racing with all the things I have to get through today. We're only one week into the school semester, and classes have started with an intensity I wasn't counting on. I guess no one ever said being a senior would be easy.

"You done?" Grady stands, grabbing my plate and rinsing it off.

"Thanks, man." I top up with my third coffee and wander into the living area to find The Punisher blowing shit up and Wily snoring in the armchair. His head is tipped back, his mouth wide open, and the laptop is precariously perched on his lap.

I race forward and catch it before it hits the wood, placing it on the coffee table, then plunking down beside Carson.

He grunts and pushes his shades a little higher up his nose.

"How hungover are you?" I mutter.

"Bad enough that I don't want to fucking talk about it."

"'Kay." I nod. "So, no *LOUD NOISES, THEN*?" I shout into his ear.

"You fucker," he hisses, trying to punch me in the arm. I laugh, flicking his fist away and getting into a short tussle on the couch as Carson tries and fails to maim me.

I shove him away with a palm to his forehead, and he lunges back, growling like a grumpy dog, his fist raised in the air. I block for the attack, laughing at the look on his face... then we both go still as the front door slams shut.

Wily jerks and sits up with a start, blinking toward the archway just as Tyrell stalks in with a pissed-off scowl... and a milkshake-soaked shirt.

"Whoa." Grady laughs, standing next to him and doing nothing to try and smother the sound. "What happened to you?"

"Donita happened!" he barks. "I was just trying to do the right thing, and..." He spreads his arms wide.

Carson snickers, then snorts and starts howling like a hyena—the guy has a weird-ass laugh. Tyrell glares at him, which makes me laugh, too, and soon Wily—the most sympathetic guy in the house—is doing his barking laugh that sounds more seal than human.

"Sorry, dude." Wily struggles to talk. "But that's epic. A milkshake thrown in your face? That's like rom-com movie level shit, man."

And only Wily would know what the hell people do in rom-coms.

"Why'd you break up with her again?" Grady asks,

taking a seat on the beanbag while Tyrell strips off his jacket and shirt.

Throwing them onto the wooden floor with a huff, he scrubs a hand down his face and mutters, "Because she was getting too clingy. I don't want to be with a girl who needs to know where I am every second of every fucking day."

Carson hisses. "I hear ya, dude. That shit is creepy. This is why I don't do girlfriends."

"There's nothing wrong with having a girlfriend." Grady rolls his eyes.

"That's because yours is perfect," Wily argues. "She's pretty and sweet, and she respects your training and game schedule. She doesn't ride you about not having enough time for her, and when you're together, you enjoy each other's company. If we all had girlfriends like that, we'd be dating too."

"Fuck off. No, we wouldn't," Carson grumbles.

Wily gives him the finger, then looks to me. "Back me up here, Zan-Man."

"Teah's great." I lift my chin toward Grady. "You're a lucky guy. But girls like that are few and far between. I prefer to play it safe and just keep things light. A casual hookup every now and then is enough for me."

He points at me. "You say that now, but just wait until you fall in love."

My stomach clenches and I sniff, hoping no one notices. I arrived at Nolan U my sophomore year and left my past as far behind me as I could. I haven't told these guys shit about my fuckup of a college freshman year... or how things ended with my high school sweetheart.

Carson groans, whipping off his shades and squinting into the light. His hazel gaze is intense. "Love is bullshit, Grady. Those feelings don't last. Not for both of you, anyway. Someone always fucks it up." He turns to Wily and winces. "Remember last year... the serenader who wouldn't let go?"

Wily runs a hand through his hair, his blue eyes popping wide. "Oh shit, yeah! Damn, that was awkward."

I can't help a laugh. "If she'd been able to sing on key, it wouldn't have been so painful."

"She ruined 'I Will Always Love You' for me," Tyrell mutters, and then we all crack up and start hassling him for being obsessed with Whitney Houston.

"Laugh all you want, you cheese dicks. Whitney was the best damn singer this world has ever known." He plunks down onto the couch and mumbles under his breath, "Now that is a woman I'd never break up with."

"Yeah, I'm sure if she was still alive, she'd be all over your, dude." Grady smirks.

Tyrell tips his head back, nestling it into the cushions with a groan. "Breakups fucking suck."

"Whether you're the dumper or the dumpee, it's always shit," Wily agrees.

Tyrell sighs. "I've been both, and that's why I was trying to be so nice about it with Donita, but she flipped out. Went full-blown psycho on my ass." He clicks his tongue and sits back up. "Women ain't worth it." Giving Carson a light slap on the arm, he bobs his head. "I'm going your way, bro. Casual hookups only from now on."

I nod. "It definitely makes it easier."

Grady's shaking his head, disagreeing with me as he

no doubt thinks about his hot sorority girl and how great she is.

Yeah, well, it's not like that for all of us.

A scorching memory burns through the back of my brain, but I shake it off. I can't go there.

"I'm here to play football," I grit out, begging images of Sienna not to devour me. "I'm not gonna waste my time on romantic bullshit."

My nostrils flare, my knee starting to bob as I remind myself how brutal romance can be. I'm not gonna put myself through that again. I've only ever loved one girl, and she broke my heart with a fucking sledgehammer.

FOUR YEARS AGO...

"WE MET"

CHAPTER 2
ZANDER

My senior year of high school starts next week, and I am pumped. Scouts from a few different colleges came to our games last year, and I caught their attention. If I can have the season of my life, then I'll have offers coming in from all over the place. Brighton College seems interested, which is the closest to home. Mom's got her fingers crossed for that one—I'll only be thirty minutes out of town. Dad and I also sent highlight videos to a college in Texas, one in Colorado, and he *made me* send one to his alma mater—Kelsey University. I'm not totally opposed to going there, I guess. I just want to follow my own path, not be trailing in my father's wake, but it's not like I can say that to him.

At the end of the day, I just wanna play football, and I don't really care where I do that...as long as I get plenty of time on the field. If I can shine at college, my ultimate dream of playing for the NFL could become a reality.

And that... would be fucking awesome.

I'm pretty fired up over that idea right now, which is why I nearly didn't come to this party tonight.

But Noah wouldn't shut up about it, so I agreed.

He had some good points, one of them being that Olivia Monroe's the richest girl in school and her house is palatial. I went to a few parties last year at her old house and thought that was grand, but her family upgraded over the summer, and you don't pass up a chance to see what luxury living looks like.

They even have rose-shaped soaps in the bathroom. Apparently. I haven't gone yet, but that was one of the first things Noah did when he got here. Who knows what other rooms he checked out at the same time, but he came back looking all triumphant.

"What?" I asked him, but he just shook his head with sparkling eyes.

"This place is fucking awesome. Her parents must be so loaded."

"I know, right?" Kyle breathed, his eyes bulging. "I swear her dad must shit money before breakfast every morning."

Great, now I'm picturing Mr. Monroe taking a dump, his face straining as he pops out a roll of hundies.

"Classy," I mutter.

"What?" Kyle laughs. "It's true!"

I shake my head and move to the keg, pouring my friends a beer and handing them out until I'm left with one in my hand.

I sip the amber brew and remind my buddies that I can't be out too late. Even though my parents are divorced, they still tell each other fucking *everything* when it comes to their kids. My dad is riding me hard this year, and I'd rather avoid another nuclear meltdown. The guy has a short fuse. I appreciate his commitment, wanting to get me into the best college possible, but it's kind of suffocating. Thank God it's my week with Mom. If I was staying at his place, he probably wouldn't have let me go out tonight. I mean, he couldn't have really stopped me, but sometimes it's just easier to give in and avoid the drama.

"So, which chicks am I hitting on at this party?" Kyle scans the room, and I can't help joining him, taking in boobs in pretty tank tops and faces enhanced with perfectly applied makeup. The kinds of girls who attend these parties go all out. Who knows how many hours they spent preening before they got here, but I'm not complaining.

My eyes track past Giselle, then over to Amanda before she moves out of the way and I'm staring at a blonde goddess I don't even recognize.

The air in my lungs turns soft and wispy as I drink her in.

She's got a stunning smile, her blue eyes sparkling as she grins at Olivia, then takes another sip of beer. She's wearing a skintight miniskirt with this pale pink tank top that shows off her belly button and toned stomach.

Holy shit, she's fire.

"Who is that?" I end up whispering the words and no doubt sounding like a love-drunk moron.

"Who?" Noah leans in, trying to follow my line of sight.

"The blonde with the killer tits?" Kyle asks.

"Yeah." I bob my head but frown at him. "Stop looking at her tits, man."

"It's hard not to. Look at them all snugged up in that top. Damn, I'd love to peel that thing right off her body and—"

I slap his chest with the back of my hand and growl, "Stop talking."

Noah laughs and cuts in. "I've seen her around this summer, but I can't remember her name. She's friends with Olivia."

"How have I not seen her?" Because I can't take my eyes off her right now, and I would *remember* a face that beautiful. "Does she go to our school?"

"Yeah, she will be. She starts next week. Junior, I think," Kyle tells me.

"What's her name?" Noah mutters.

"I think it's a mountain range, isn't it?"

"What?" I turn to look at Kyle.

"I'm serious. It's like Andes or something."

"It's not Andes," Noah scoffs, lightly whacking Kyle's head. "It's like Sarah or something."

"No, it's not," Kyle argues, rubbing his head before landing a punch on Noah's arm. "It's like Sierra or something. That's a mountain range, right?"

Noah rolls his eyes. "Her name is not a mountain range, you moron."

Ignoring my idiot friends, I snag Jayne's arm as she walks past. "Hey, who's the new girl?" I lift my chin toward the blonde beauty.

She glances over her shoulder, then gives me a knowing smirk. "Pretty, isn't she?"

I give her a "well, duh" look, and she cracks up laughing. "Her name's Sienna, Romeo." With a little wink, she glides past us, and Kyle starts looking all triumphant.

"See, I told you it was a mountain range."

I give Noah a quizzical frown before we both turn to Kyle.

"What?" He glances between us like *we're* the idiots.

With a soft snicker, I shake my head, and Noah mutters, "Yeah, want to point out the Sienna Ranges to me on a map, genius?"

Kyle glares at us both, pulling out his phone and getting all huffy and indignant. "I'll prove it, you little fuckers." We wait for his thumbs to fly over the screen before he stills, goes kind of red, and then shoves his phone back into his pocket. "I hate you both," he murmurs, and I can't help snorting out a laugh while Noah cracks up and slaps him on the back.

"Next time, buddy. I'm sure you'll be right once in your life."

Kyle growls in his throat, then gulps down a few more mouthfuls of beer while Noah tries and fails to stop laughing.

I've managed because my focus is now back on Sienna.

Sienna.

Pretty name.

Perfect for a girl like her. It's got this foreign, kind of elusive quality to it, and it seems to sum her up somehow.

I don't know where she comes from or if she has an accent or... anything about her.

I just know I have to talk to her, and standing around

laughing at what a clueless douche Kyle is won't help me do that.

Downing the last of my Solo cup, I hand it to Noah and softly murmur, "I'm going in."

He snickers. "Good luck, lover boy."

I walk away from their hassles. I'm not usually the guy who goes and chats up a girl. They tend to come to me. I'm not being arrogant—it's just the way it is.

I'm no party animal or ladies' man, but being the star quarterback on our school team gives me status, and for some reason, girls think I'm cool. I try to be nice to them when they talk to me. I smile and laugh the way I know I should, but with football and studying, it's not like I have time to date and mess around. So I tend to keep things light, and girls get annoyed with me, calling me aloof and arrogant.

I don't give a shit what they think about me. Football's my life. Nothing else matters.

But I might just make an exception tonight...

As I weave through the crowd, my insides jitter with fiery anticipation. There's something kind of thrilling about making the first move.

I can't go screwing this up.

Because of all the girls I've ever seen or met, this one is special. I can already tell. Something inside me is calling, like a voice buried deep within that's just been waiting for this moment.

I'm three steps away when she glances up and sees me coming.

Her blue eyes are so vibrant, and they round just a little when they spot me. Her glossy lips part, her pale skin flushing pink seconds before I stop right in front of her.

"Hey." I smile, my mouth tipping up at the corner.

Shit, is my smile cool enough, or do I look like a dork?

I clear my throat, shoving my hands into my letterman jacket pockets and hoping she's into athletes.

She's still staring at me, her cheeks turning even redder.

"I haven't seen you around before. You're new, right?" I lean forward, aware of the excited gazes all around me. The girls are being so fucking obvious as they watch me make my move.

"I'm Zander. Zander Donahue."

She doesn't need your last name, you douche!

"And you're Sienna, right?"

She nods, finally entering the conversation. I grin, leaning a little closer as she opens her mouth...

And throws up all over me.

CHAPTER 3
SIENNA

Oh shit. Please tell me I didn't just throw up on Zander Donohue!

I've only been crushing on him since the first moment I saw him.

He's only the hottest guy in Everett. Probably the hottest guy in Idaho. Correction: the world.

It's not like I don't dream about him every night and obsess over how I'm going to meet him.

I blink, my hazy brain struggling to comprehend what I'm seeing.

I think I'm looking at my puke on his shirt, which is now sticking to his extremely cut and muscly chest. He's gaping down at the mess, and I'm just waiting for him to say, "You're gross!" and walk away, never to speak to me again.

"I'm sorry," I blubber, letting out a drunk hiccup and nearly upchucking all over again.

I slap a hand over my mouth and sway on my feet.

"Are you gonna be sick again?" He rests his hand lightly on my elbow.

I shake my head, still swaying like a stiff breeze could knock me over. Still holding a hand over my mouth and begging my body to behave.

Damn you, alcohol! I'm never drinking again!

"Come on." Zander lightly takes my arm, turning to someone and asking, "Where's the bathroom?"

"This way." It's a girl. I recognize her voice.

Olivia! It's my new friend Olivia.

Save me! I silently beg her. *I just puked on the guy I like! Help!*

But she can't hear me... probably because I'm not saying any of those words out loud.

Wait, am I?

I blink, shaking my head and tripping over in these heels.

Why am I even wearing heels?

"Whoa." A strong arm catches me, securing me around the waist.

"I don't feel very good," I rasp.

"Yeah, I can tell." His voice is deep and soft, kind of husky. My insides tremble. I've found my new favorite sound. "You ever been drunk before?"

"No." I hiccup again, and he makes us walk a little faster.

"In here," Olivia says.

I force my floppy head to look her way and give her a smile that I'm sure looks dopey. "Thanks, Livvy Lou."

"Oh my gosh," she mutters. "Seriously, how much did you drink, Sen? You're such a lightweight."

"I had to," I whine.

"Okay. Here we go." Strong hands direct me to the toilet, catching me when my ankle turns again. "I gotcha." He slows my crumpling descent to the floor, catching my hair and holding it back as my next hiccup turns into a puke explosion.

"Oh, gross. I can't." Olivia starts dry heaving, spinning on her heel and rushing out of the bathroom.

A hand lightly rubs my shoulder. "It's okay." That soft, husky voice is in my ear again, and I shiver. "You cold?"

He doesn't wait for my answer, shrugging his jacket off and draping it over my shoulders before passing me a wad of toilet paper.

"Let me get you some water." He makes sure I'm steady before walking to the sink and grabbing a glass. "I think this is clean." He inspects it under the light, giving it a quick rinse before filling it.

I'm not sure how I'm supposed to hold it, and nearly tell him that, but he crouches down in front of me, his smile gentle as he helps me drink.

He's got nice lips. Luscious. Full. I bet they feel amazing.

I can't take my eyes off his beautiful face as I sip down the cold liquid.

It dribbles off my bottom lip, and he swipes it with his finger.

How is he not running out of the room right now?

I glance at his shirt, my nose wrinkling.

"Yeah, let's get rid of this mess," he mutters, standing tall and stripping off his shirt. I gape at his naked torso.

Holy shit, I was right. He is Hercules.

My gaze tracks his perfect form, every ridge of his body chiseled to perfection. Olivia says he works really hard at the gym and on the field. Apparently he never eats sugar and is pretty serious about this whole football thing.

Whatever he's doing, it's working.

I watched him practice the other day, and I was impressed. Not that I know anything about football, but he was great at passing the ball—it went so far!—and I like how hot he looks in those football tights.

"Your body is beautiful," I slur, drinking him in like I want to lick his skin off.

He smirks but looks kind of awkward, like he doesn't know what to do with the compliment.

"I'm serious." I blink up at him. "You're, like, sooooo beautiful." I reach up as if to touch him, maybe even brush my fingers across those pecs and down the line between his ab muscles.

But my hand kind of gives up, feeling nothing but thin air before flopping against my thigh.

Crouching back down, he brushes the hair back off my face. "So, not too great with your liquor, huh?"

I snicker and shake my head. "This is my first time drinking, really. I mean, Dad lets me have a few sips of his beer sometimes, but this party's a free-for-all. I have no idea how many beers I've had. Plus, there were those little shot things Becky gave me. They burn." I wince and then start giggling... or am I crying?

"Yeah, I bet." His finger is soft as he tucks my hair behind my ear.

"I didn't mean to get drunk," I blubber.

Okay, so I'm crying, then.

This just keeps getting better and better, doesn't it?

"But I was so nervous to be here," I try to explain. "And then Liv dared me, and I needed some liquid courage." My words tumble together. I'm not sure if he can even understand me, but he lets out a soft laugh.

"Liquid courage, huh? And why were you so nervous?"

"Because they dared me to talk to you." My eyes go round, and I grip his forearm. "And that's scary because I like you so much."

"You do?" He blinks, obviously surprised.

I gape at him. "How could I not? You're Zander. I've liked you for forever."

His eyebrows wrinkle. "Didn't you just move here?"

"I've been here like four weeks." My words are lagging, and trying to talk is like dragging cotton balls out of my mouth, but for some reason, I just keep going. "I saw you in the mall my first week here, and I was like... he's hot. And then I spotted you again at the movies, and I was like... yup, still hot. So I started looking for you everywhere I went... and you kept popping up." I flick my finger through the air with a giggle. "It helps that I was looking in all the right places. Olivia knows your hang-outs and where you guys practice." I'm trying to point at him, but my hand is kind of droopy. I swing it back to point at me as I lay my head on the edge of the toilet seat. "So, Olivia knows that I've got, like, a mondo crush on you, and she was like 'Let's throw a party, and you can catch his eye and flirt and stuff.' She tells me you're nice, too, so you're like the whole package, and I can tell. I've been watching you, Zander Donohue." My lips curl into a tipsy smile. "And I like what I see."

Zander lets out another laugh. "So, you threw this party for me, huh?"

"Of course." My tongue feels thick and floppy as I lick my lips. "But I'm not very good at flirting, and I didn't want to sound like an idiot or anything." I rub my nose and blink. My eyelids feel heavy, my brain starting to float. "So, I thought I'd have a few drinks to take the edge off."

"Maybe one too many, huh?"

"Yeah, maybe," I murmur, then blink again, the world going fuzzy. "Do you think he'll like me?"

"Who?" the husky voice asks.

"Zander."

There's a pause, and I open my eyes as wide as I can, the blurry image in front of me shifting as I start to fall forward.

Something solid catches me, and I let out a soft sigh, a black fog taking me away as I float into oblivion against something that's both firm and gentle.

CHAPTER 4
ZANDER

She fell asleep against my chest, her open mouth leaving a fine coat of drool against my left pec. Awesome.

Considering how many bodily fluids this girl has left on me tonight, I'm a little surprised that I'm still sitting here cradling her against me... but I just can't help it.

There's something about her. It could be the drunk confessions, which were plain adorable. It could have been the hungry way she looked at me, although that was kind of disconcerting. Or maybe it's the fact that there's something sweet about her smile. There's something playful and intoxicating about the curl of her lips.

I need to get to know this girl.

"Has she stopped puking?" Olivia eases the door open like she's approaching an armed bomb.

"Yeah, she fell asleep."

The door punches open, the muffled music rolling into the room with a loud wave of clarity. I wince at the thick beat as Olivia rushes toward us, crouching down to check on her friend. "Shit, she doesn't have alcohol poisoning or anything, does she? Like, she's legit breathing, right?" She holds her fingers near Sienna's mouth and sags with relief when she feels her friend breathing. "Thank God," she murmurs. "I had no idea she was such a lightweight. She just wanted something to take the edge off, and I didn't realize she'd been downing so much."

I give Olivia a dry look, not sure if I believe her or not. The girl is known to party.

"What! It's the truth!" She slaps my arm, then stands with a huff. "Can you help me get her upstairs, please?" Her tone is terse, her pointed glare leaving no room for argument.

Moving carefully, I adjust Sienna in my arms, then stand with her against me.

"I'll get you a clean shirt too." Olivia's nose wrinkles as she looks into the bathroom sink. "I'm gonna burn that one."

I roll my eyes. "It's only puke. I can just wash it."

"Gross, no. I'm getting you a clean one." She leads me upstairs, and I lay Sienna down on Olivia's bed. "Wait, she doesn't have puke on her, does she?"

I look Sienna over, trying not to appreciate how hot her curves are while I look for spots of vomit, but... "I'm pretty sure I was the only one who got hit."

"Oh good. I don't want her ruining my comforter."

Again, I roll my eyes as Olivia walks out of the room to find me a clean shirt.

Taking a careful seat on the edge of the bed, I gaze down at Sienna's pretty face. Not to sound like a sap, but she's got an angelic quality about her, and I need to get to know this girl. I can feel it in my very core. She's something special.

Which is probably why I spend my weekend thinking about her... wishing I had her number so I could check on her when I woke up on Sunday morning. I nearly popped over to Olivia's house to offer Sienna a ride home, but Dad swung by Mom's place and made me help him with yard work. My parents have been divorced since my older sister left for college, but Dad still comes over every few weeks to help maintain the house. I'm not sure why. Maybe he does it out of guilt for leaving in the first place. Or maybe he still has a thing for Mom. Whatever the reason, it's always painful, because he turns me into his personal lackey, and I sweat up a storm being bossed around on my one day off while also getting interrogated about football and what I'm going to do with my future.

I go to bed in a shitty mood on Sunday night, and the only thing to ease my temper is the thought that the next morning, I'll get to talk to a blue-eyed blonde with a smile that could knock a guy off his feet.

The second I get to school, I start scanning for her and spot her near the junior lockers, sorting her books and looking fine in a pair of fitted jeans and an oversized sweater that's hanging off her shoulder.

Noah's in the middle of telling me about his epic *Final Fantasy* gaming session, and I walk away from him as if drawn by some invisible power I have no control over.

"Dude, I'm in the middle of a story here!" he calls to my back, but I keep walking, ignoring how rude I'm being because...

She's right in front of me.

31

"Hey." I smile down at her, enjoying the hint of vanilla I'm catching and the way her blonde hair falls over her shoulders. The light from the upper windows is turning it a sparkling gold, and her eyes are so damn...

Well, actually they're kind of staring at me like she's terrified and has no idea why I'm talking to her.

"Um... hi?" She licks her lips before glancing over her shoulder as if searching for backup.

I take a small step back and shove my hands into my pockets, hating the idea that I'm making her uneasy. I thought we were vibing at the party, but maybe I was reading the signals wrong. She was drunk off her ass. Was everything she said in the bathroom total bullshit?

Clearing my throat, I try for a casual, light tone while scrambling for a way to bail without looking like a total douche. "So, how's it going? Any first day jitters, or are you holding up okay?"

"Uh..." Her blue eyes dart around my face before dropping down to the book bag clutched in her hand. "I'm... I'm good?" Her eyebrows wrinkle, and she glances up at me like she's confused by the fact that I'm standing here asking about her.

Scratching the back of my head, I let out a soft, awkward laugh and just come out with it. "Why are you looking at me like that?"

She's obviously completely mystified and slightly terrified by the question.

I start to worry that I did something wrong. Why is she so freaked out right now? What the fuck did Olivia tell her I did at the party?

Anger starts to simmer, but it morphs to confusion when Sienna quietly asks, "Why are you talking to me?"

"Why—" An awkward laugh punches out of me. "Well... we met at Olivia's party, and I thought I'd come over and see—"

Her eyes bulge. "We met at her party?"

"Yeah."

"On Saturday?"

"Yeah."

"And I spoke to you?" Her voice has gone all soft and wispy, the color draining from her face.

Oh shit. She doesn't remember a thing.

"Did Olivia not tell you?"

"No." Her eyes dart to the right, and I turn to see Olivia hovering nearby.

Olivia winces and mumbles, "I thought you'd die of humiliation, so I kinda didn't say anything."

Sienna's breath catches before she stumbles over her words, "Why would I... why... why would I die of humiliation?"

It's impossible to keep my laughter in check, but I do my best when she looks at me with bulging eyes, her cheeks turning from white to bright red.

I cringe and admit, "You kind of threw up on me."

"No." Her expression bunches with horror. "No, no, no, no." Covering her face, she groans into her hands. "Kill me now."

My laughter is light as I softly reassure her, "Seriously, it's fine. I'm just glad you're okay."

"Uh-huh." She nods, but she still has her face covered.

Lightly taking her wrists, I try to pull her hands away, but she resists me, and I have to let go and just admire the shape of her fingers instead. I like the ring on her middle finger. It's a blue opal and matches the color of her eyes. "You obviously don't remember much, huh?"

"No." Her words are muffled. "I mean, I woke up in Olivia's bed, no idea how I got there." Her hands fall away, but she keeps her eyes on the floor. "I had this monster headache, and my brain was, like, blank. Olivia just said the party went well, I got completely shit-faced, but she assured me that I *didn't* embarrass myself." She glances up to throw a hot glare at her friend.

Olivia, never one to apologize, actually has the decency to mutter, "Sorry. I was just trying to protect you"

Sienna's delicate nostrils flare, her jaw clenching as she looks back down at the floor again.

Leaning my shoulder against the locker beside hers, I lower my voice and move into her space so she's the only one who can hear me. "You didn't embarrass yourself."

"I totally did. I threw up on you." Then she gasps and those big blue eyes are staring at me, once again wide with horror. "Did I say anything to you? Before I puked?"

I shrug. "Not really."

"Oh." Her expression wrinkles, and then she nods. "Okay. Well..." Her head bobs some more. "Good. That's good."

"You spoke to me after you threw up, though."

She goes pale again, and my lips pull into a grin. I probably shouldn't be enjoying this so much, but...

"What'd I, um...?" She licks her lips again, obviously steeling herself. "What'd I say?"

I flick my fingers through the air, taking pity on her and going for a casual brush-off. "Don't worry about it. Not a big deal."

"No." She snatches my wrist, her grip surprisingly strong considering how skinny her wrists and fingers are. "What'd I say? And you have to tell me the truth."

Her voice is so strong and adamant.

Something stirs in my chest, an unfamiliar sensation that... I kinda like.

Looking her in the eye, I study her expression and softly ask, "You sure you wanna know?"

"Yes, please. I hate it when people lie to me, even if they're trying to protect me, so please, just say it." She swallows. "How badly did I humiliate myself?"

"You didn't." I tip my head, still hyperaware of the fact that she's holding my wrist. I like the feel of her fingers on my skin.

"Zander." She closes her eyes, then grits out the rest. "What did I say?"

Letting out a soft sigh, I finally give in. "Okay, you..." I sigh again, then just blurt it out as gently as I can. "You told me you liked me and that you've liked me ever since you saw me. You keep finding excuses to watch me and—"

"I swear I'm not a stalker." She whimpers and covers her face again.

I grin, lightly nudging her hand away so I can look into those sparkly blue eyes again. "You told me the party was put together so that you and I could meet, and that your friend dared you to speak to me and that's why you got drunk. Because you were nervous."

35

A little whine pops out of her throat, her face crumpling into a cringe that's just plain adorable. I love how red her cheeks go.

"You know you don't have to be nervous to talk to me." I can't resist brushing my finger over her ear like I did the night of the party.

She doesn't flinch away from my touch. Instead, her lips pull into a self-deprecating smile. "I'm surprised you're not running away screaming."

"Why would I do that? A pretty girl likes me." I wink and she goes still, like she can't believe I just said that... and the first bell trills. "I'll see you around, Sienna. Have a good first day."

She lets out a soft breath that could also be a giggle, maybe, and then I try to play it cool, sauntering down the hallway toward Noah and Kyle.

For a second, I wonder if I should have offered to walk her to class. Maybe she needs help finding her homeroom. I spin back to see what she's doing, and my chest spasms when I notice her leaning against the locker. Her eyes are closed, and there's this dreamy smile on her face.

She's swooning. She's actually *swooning*!

Talk about an ego boost.

I stop in my tracks, spinning to face her properly and drinking in the view.

That's when her eyes pop open. Her gaze hits mine, and I can't help a smile as she flushes and jerks tall, quickly turning to face her locker and sorting out her books.

Olivia and a few of the other girls move in, no doubt

to analyze every syllable of our conversation, and I wander off to class already knowing that my senior year of high school has taken a life-changing turn.

"WE FLIRTED"

CHAPTER 5
SIENNA

Zander was so freaking nice to me, it was impossible not to like him even more than I already did. I threw up on him, and he told me it wasn't a big deal. I drunkenly humiliated myself with loose lips, and he didn't judge me for it.

I like him so much it hurts... but it's been nearly two weeks since the party, and we still haven't done anything more than casually say hi when we cross each other's paths at school.

In fairness to him, he's a busy guy. Football is king around here, and I've been forced to learn the ins and outs of the game. Olivia's been teaching me what she knows, and even my dad helped me out.

See, I'm not your standard all-American girl. My parents are... well, they're nomads. They've always struggled to stay in one place for long, and I spent my early childhood growing up around the world. We lived out of a camper van, traveling through Europe for the first three years of my life. Then we spent a few years checking out

Asia, and I was homeschooled in places like Chiang Mai, Hanoi, Bali, and Kuala Lumpur. We then did a stint in the Pacific Islands, where I got myself a tan playing on the beaches of Fiji and Samoa, before we finally headed back to the States. I was hitting puberty, and my parents decided it was time for me to experience "normal" life for a while.

I have no idea what possessed them to do this, because adjusting to life stateside was freaking hard. I was the weirdo kid with an accent that no one could place and more life experience than all the kids I hung out with. They just didn't get me. And I struggled to understand them too.

I begged my parents to hit the road again, but Dad was enjoying living next door to his best friend, so we stuck it out... until the chance to live in New York came along. By then, I'd made some friends and was finally starting to enjoy life. Being uprooted was just plain mean, but I survived that, and I'd survive life in Idaho too.

Plus, my parents promised to stay until I graduate, which means I don't have to stress about being pulled out of school halfway through this year.

It means I have until June to make something happen with Zander Donohue.

Some would argue that I'm just setting myself up for heartache. He'll be leaving school at the end of this year... but thanks to some sleuthing, I've heard the coaches at Brighton College are interested in him. And Brighton's like the next town over. A thirty-minute drive is nothing.

I'm choosing to be positive about this thing.

And if the eye flirting Zander and I have been doing

over the past few days is anything to go by, I'm in a good position here.

He thinks I'm pretty; I can tell that much.

Why he hasn't asked me out yet, I'm not sure. I mean, I guess I could always ask him, but that's kind of terrifying, so I'll just keep getting into his line of sight.

It's been less than two weeks, Sen. Give the guy a break.

But twelve days feels like a millennium when you like a guy and you think he likes you back. I mean, right?

I'll just have to keep making my smiles brighter whenever we walk past each other.

I'll just have to keep throwing out flirty comments whenever he's close enough to hear me.

He likes it when I do that. I can tell.

Shuffling in the stands, I rub my arms, trying to stay warm as the football game unfolds before us.

Zander's on the field, getting in position to take the ball and... throw it down the field.

"Yes!" I make a fist, tensing as I watch the wide receiver chase the ball down and catch it just twenty yards from the end zone. "Woo-hoo!" I punch the air, jumping to my feet with the rest of the crowd.

Man, I love Friday nights.

This is my first Friday night game, but I just know they'll be addictive.

I love that this is a home game.

I love this crowd.

Olivia giggles, giving me a sideways hug. "Your man is on fire tonight."

"He's not her man," Becky says testily. "They haven't even gone on one date."

"Oh please. With the amount of eye sex these two are having, it's just a matter of time."

"Eye sex?" I grab her jacket sleeve. "We're not having eye sex."

"Whatever you say, hon." She pats my hand and starts laughing at me. "You're so red right now."

"I'm not having eye sex with Zander Donohue." I flush, covering my no doubt neon cheeks.

Becky snorts and shakes her head, obviously agreeing with Olivia. I turn to Emily for backup, but she's no help. Her eyebrows are wiggling up and down, and the smirk on her lips tells me I'm a fool for not realizing that is exactly what I've been doing.

"You want him so bad," Olivia starts singing and doing this seductive dance that's catching the eye of everyone around us.

"Stop it," I hiss, wrapping my arm around her. "You're killing me."

She cackles and kisses my cheek.

"So, when are you actually going to do something about it?" Becky gives me a pointed look while the team sets up for their next play.

I keep my eyes on the field, hoping to avoid the question. I have no idea what to do about it. If Zander likes me as much as I like him, he would have asked me out already, right?

So now I'm worried that if I ask him first, he'll just say he's not interested or it's not a good time for him. Ugh—I've heard that one before.

In ninth grade, I plucked up the courage to ask Stephen Tanaki to the school dance, and he just winced and murmured, "Sorry. Now's not really a good time for me."

What the hell did that mean?

Everyone within earshot started laughing at me, and I swore I would never initiate a date again. And I'm still not sure I'm willing to break that vow, even if it is Zander Donohue, the guy I've liked more than any other guy in my entire life!

"Touchdown!" Emily yells, jumping to her feet and cheering for her brother, Noah. "Good job!" She's clapping and laughing, turning to spot her parents in the stand behind us and giving them a wave. Her mom looks so proud right now.

I smile and cheer along with the crowd, my eyes trained on Zander as he takes off his helmet and runs to the edge of the field. The team is jumping around and slapping one another on the helmets and shoulders and butts. Seriously, boys are weird.

"It's halftime. Let's go grab a hot cider." Becky stands, ordering us up, but my eyes are still trained on the field as the team makes their way to the locker room.

Zander looks up, maybe sensing my stare, and I boldly watch him, my lips curling into a smile. He grins back, then stops on the track, hollering up to me, "Wait for me after the game!"

I point to myself, walking down the stairs and making sure I'm not imagining this.

He laughs. "Yeah, you, bright eyes!" Then, with the sexiest wink ever given to anyone, he picks up his pace and disappears down the tunnel.

With a gasp, I spin to find my friends watching me with various expressions of triumph.

"You guys just saw that, right?" I practically squeal.

"Sure did." Becky smirks. "Looks like the eye sex might be coming to an end."

I give her a confused frown.

Emily wiggles her eyebrows again. "Time for the real sex to begin."

My lips part. "But I'm not... I don't want... I mean, I'm not ready for that."

The girls crack up laughing, and Olivia runs down to wrap her arm around my shoulders. "Don't worry. We're only teasing. Zander's not just into you for the sex. I can tell he really likes you."

"You think so?" My stomach churns.

"Of course. He never asks girls out. He's all about football, you know? But he's making an exception for you." She gives me a heartfelt smile. "That's special, Sen."

I nod, my insides twirling as I imagine what awaits me after the game.

CHAPTER 6
ZANDER

We won!

We fucking won!

And damn it feels good.

"Bears! Bears! Bears!" the crowd chants as we finally leave the field. Mom leans down from the stands, and like the good boy I am, I walk over to let her hug me. She wraps her arms around my neck so tight I think I'm going to choke, and Dad is right behind her, patting my back and telling me that I did great, but there's still room for improvement.

The guy does not know how to just enjoy the win.

I shake them off me and head to the locker room, hoping they'll leave by the time I get out. I normally take my sweet time, giving them plenty of chances to go, but I'm in a hurry tonight, blitzing through a shower and throwing on fresh clothes while the coaches continue to congratulate each other and the guys throw triumphant comments and hassles back and forth.

I tune them all out, towel-drying my hair and fighting a grin...

Because a bright-eyed girl with the best smile is waiting for me.

Holy shit, I can't believe I just yelled that up to her, but she was looking at me in that way she always does, and I couldn't resist. She came to the game! And I know she only did that because of me. I've asked around, found out what I could. She's not a football girl. Apparently she's been trying to learn the game, and Emily told Noah that she's only doing it because she has the biggest crush on me.

I've been wanting to ask her out ever since the party, but between practice, studying, managing two parents, and making it to work on time, I haven't wanted to ask Sienna out only to have to bail on her.

But it's my monthly weekend off work, and I want to make the most of it.

Shit, I should have asked her out with more time to spare. What if she's not free tomorrow?

My gut twists as I finish drying my hair and rush to pull my jacket on.

"Where's the fire?" The assistant coach laughs at me.

"He's got himself a pretty girl waiting in the parking lot, Coach." Noah rats me out, and the entire locker room starts hassling me.

I glare at my friend, shouldering my bag and running out before someone tells me I shouldn't be trying to fit a girl into my life as well.

This isn't just any girl. Exceptions need to be made.

I've been watching her for two weeks, trying to talk to

her between classes, smiling back whenever she catches my eye. And tonight's my chance to finally do something about all this damn pining.

"Zander." Dad's voice catches my attention the second I hit the asphalt. Dammit.

I force a smile. "Hey."

"Great game tonight."

"Yeah, you said before." I point my thumb at the field.

The corners of his eyes narrow, and my insides are already squirming before he asks, "Where are you off to now?"

"Um..."

"Oh, go easy on him, Brett," Mom butts in. "He's allowed to blow off a little steam."

"I just don't want him going crazy. I know what guys are like after a game."

"He'll be sensible." Mom pats my chest. "Won't you, baby?"

"Yeah, of course." I clench my jaw. The tension riding through me is headache inducing.

Dad's eyes are like laser beams, burning right through my skull. "Fine. Go and have some fun celebrating with the boys, but I want you home by midnight."

"He's staying with me tonight, and he can be home by one." Mom gives my father a saccharine smile.

He narrows his eyes at her before huffing and spinning away, grumbling over his shoulder, "He's mine next week."

I sigh while Mom gives me a glum smile. "Ignore him. He's always testy after a tough week at work."

How the hell does she know what his week was like?

I so don't get my parents.

All I know is that this week-on/week-off bullshit is exhausting. I go from one pressure point to the other. In Dad's house, it's like being at military school. And Mom's place is manipulation central.

Thank God I'll be living in a dorm next year. Yes, even if I go to Brighton and it's only thirty minutes away, I *will* be living in a dorm!

Mom pulls me down so she can kiss my cheek, then tells me to have fun. "Turn the porch light off when you get in, baby. I'll already be asleep."

"Will do." I straighten my jacket, relieved she didn't ask for details about where I'm going tonight.

Both my parents assume I'm heading to Noah's for video games and pizza.

But...

Spinning on my heel, I head toward my car, my smile growing a mile wide when I spot a twitchy blonde perched against my back bumper.

Olivia is hovering nearby, obviously keeping an eye out for me, and as soon as I'm within hearing distance, I catch, "Okay, sweets. Have fun."

She gives me a little wave, then scoots off, leaving me alone with a blushing Sienna.

"Hey." I grin down at her.

"Hi." She smiles back, standing tall and smoothing down her skintight jeans.

Damn, her legs are long and lean and... fire. She's fire. What I wouldn't give to skim my hand up that taut denim, round the perfect curve of her ass.

Look up, you idiot! Stop thinking about her ass!

I force my eyes back up to her face. The breeze is blowing her fine hair across her cheek. She captures it, tucking it behind her ear before I get the chance.

For some weird reason, my heart is racing.

"So..." She tips onto the edges of her blue-and-white Adidas. "You wanted me to wait for you."

"I did." I grin. "I was hoping you'd let me drive you home."

Sienna's breath catches, her bright eyes dancing like fairy lights, her voice breathy. "Okay."

"Yeah?"

"Yes, please." The most stunning smile takes over her face, and this tingle in my chest—the one I haven't been able to shake—grows with intensity.

Opening the trunk, I dump my bag in the back, then race around to the passenger door and open it for her.

"Thank you," she murmurs, another blush flaring over her smooth skin.

At least I think it's smooth. It looks flawless to me. I want to touch it. I want to brush the back of my finger down her cheek. I want to trace the line of her lips with my thumb, then pinch her chin and bring her in for a kiss.

"You okay?" She blinks up at me, and I let out this awkward laugh that's just plain embarrassing.

She giggles, her nose wrinkling. Damn, she's cute. And sweet and...

I clear my throat, closing her door and running around to the driver's side. I buckle up and grip the wheel, begging myself to stop acting like such a spaced-out moron. It's not like I can just blurt, "You're so pretty I can't think straight."

I need to pull my shit together or she'll never let me drive her home again.

Starting the engine, I turn to her with what I hope is a charming smile. "So, navigate me, lady."

She laughs as I reverse out of my spot before directing me left out of the school.

"Are you warm enough?" I ask, pumping up the heater.

"Oh, yes… I mean, no, so thank you for the heat." Her laughter is edgy and nervous, turning my insides to putty.

Turning on the stereo, I get some tunes going, and she starts to relax, bobbing her head along to the beat.

I grip the wheel, focusing on the road and getting her home safely. I've never cared so much about being a good driver, but tonight I'm on my game.

Glancing right, I steal a look at the blonde beauty beside me. Her eyes dart my way, and we flash each other a grin before quickly looking away again.

Strains of "Honeymoon Fades" by Sabrina Carpenter are filling the car. They've been playing that song so much lately. I glance Sienna's way again, enjoying the curl of her lips. She's mouthing the lyrics, then brushing her teeth over her bottom lip and making my chest do that weird clutching thing again.

Holy shit. What is this girl doing to me?

My heart hiccups as I stare at the road ahead and try to think of something to say, because we can't just drive around in silence, right?

Is that too awkward?

Is it—

"So, did you have fun playing tonight?" She breaks the silence with her sweet voice, and I feel like I take my first full breath since starting the engine.

"Uh... fun?" Football is never referred to as fun in my house. It's a goal, a commitment, a privilege.

She smiles, tipping her head to study me. "Yeah, like... it should be fun, shouldn't it? I mean, that's why you're so committed to it, right? Because you love it?"

"Yeah." I bob my head. "I've just never really thought of it like fun before. I mean, we're in it to win it, you know? That part's fun, I guess."

She gazes at me for a long beat, and my skin starts to burn. "You looked like you were enjoying it. You've got a great throw, and you seem to read the field well." Her nose wrinkles. "I don't know if I'm using the right terminology there, but from what I've researched, quarterbacks need to be smart and know the playbook really well. So, not only are you very physically amazing, but you're clever too."

"Thanks." I nod, feeling a punch of pride.

"I'm sorry you don't find it fun, though."

"I do," I quickly correct her. "I guess fun just makes it sound like we're playing a game, you know. But football's serious business."

She laughs. "I hate to break it to you, but you *are* playing a game. The *game* of football that you *play* every Friday night." She lets out a soft snort, then covers her nose, laughing quietly into her hand, while I shake my head with what has to be a blush.

"You got me." I bob my head and laugh.

Glancing at her, I enjoy the beam of the streetlights hitting her face just before I look back to the road.

"It's right at the next intersection," she murmurs. "I think." Her expression bunches. "I know I've been living here since like July, but I'm still learning this town."

"What street do you live on?"

"Chesterfield."

"Oh, that's just around the block from me."

"Really?" She perks up.

The edge of my mouth curls up on the right. "You didn't find out where I live?"

Her cheeks flare to a neon red as she bites her lower lip and winces. "As tempting as that was, I felt like it was way too stalkerish, so I wouldn't let Olivia show me, even when she offered. I instead stuck to only public stalking... like your football practices and scanning any public venue I was ever in."

My laughter comes out soft and husky. She's adorable.

"So, are we going the right way? To Chesterfield?"

Hitching my shoulder, I glance at her. "Well, we're going *a* way. A pretty long way, but..." Pausing at the lights, I turn and smile at her. "I don't mind so much."

Her teeth skim over her bottom lip as she grins at me.

So damn beautiful.

"Tell me something about yourself," I murmur. "Anything."

"Anything?" She tips her head, fighting a smile as she narrows her eyes in thought. "Um... well... I love spicy food."

"What kind of spicy?"

"Thai spicy. I spent six months living in Thailand when I was seven, and I really loved the food."

"You lived in Thailand?" My voice pitches. I've never even left the States.

"I've lived all over." Her smile grows, and there goes the rest of my night, driving the streets of Everett, listening to Sienna's travel stories and picturing her in places all over the world.

She's seen so much, experienced so many cultures. I sit there feeling out of my depth, like how can I ever be enough for this girl?

But when we finally pull up outside her house, she runs her hand down my arm. "To be honest, though, I really love being in the States. Traveling is fun, it really is, but after a while, you just want somewhere to call home, you know?" Her expression crumples. "I mean, my family is my home, but I'm talking about a house that's yours. There's something very comforting about having my own room that I can decorate. I used to sometimes wish we lived in just one place so I could carve my initials into a tree trunk or chart my height in a doorway, you know?"

"I've done both those things," I rasp. "It is pretty cool, but man... you've seen so much. That's epic."

Her blushing smile makes my chest warm.

"You're epic," she whispers. "Meeting you is epic."

I shake my head with an abashed smile. She can't go comparing me to the Eiffel Tower or Colosseum. No way am I as cool as Angkor Wat.

"It's true. Being here, starting this school... it's been the best year so far. And you're a big part of that. I didn't want to move to Everett, but then we got here, and I saw you... and I was suddenly cool with it. If anything, I was practically forcing my parents to sign some kind of declaration stating that we wouldn't be moving again until after I graduate." Her cheeks flush, and she covers them with shaking fingers. "Oh my gosh, I can't believe I just said all that. I'm not even drunk and I can't hold my tongue."

"I don't want you to hold your tongue. I like your honesty."

Her perfect nose wrinkles. "It's just so forward, and... and what if you don't feel the same way! I mean, I admitted before that I totally stalked you! How creepy is that? And now I've just confessed to my major uber-crush, and talk about pressure on you, and—"

"I do."

"What?"

"I feel the same way." I smile at her, resisting the urge to cup her cheek or run my thumb over her lower lip. "You can't tell by the fact that I'm always finding excuses to walk past you and smile at you any chance I get?"

She swivels in her seat to face me. "So, why haven't you asked me out already?"

"Because, I—" My eyes bulge, ice running through my veins as a man walks out of Sienna's front door. "Oh shit, is that your dad?"

Sienna glances over her shoulder. "Yes." Then she turns back to me with a quizzical frown. "Now, what were you saying?"

I squirm in my seat, waiting for the man to start yelling at me, demanding to know what the hell I'm doing with his daughter. I prep for the shouting, reminding myself to remain calm and assure him that my intentions are pure. I'd never do anything to disrespect his baby girl.

"Zander, are you okay?" Sienna gives me a worried frown, then turns when there's a tap on the glass. Lowering her window with a grin, she greets her father with an innocent smile while I break out in a cold sweat. "Hey, Dad."

"Hey, Blue. You guys okay out here?" Her old man crouches down. Shit, he's huge. Big, broad shoulders, and he's taller than my dad and me. I mean, I could take him if I had to, but—

"Yeah, we're just getting to know each other. This is Zander." Sienna leans back so her father can get a decent look at me.

"Hi there." He smiles, extending his hand toward me. "I'm Albin, but people just call me Al." He laughs. "You know, like the song."

I force a smile, taking his hand and wondering when he's going to start yelling at me. "Good evening, sir. We were honestly just talking."

"I know." He nods. "We've been watching you from inside the house. We were just worried you might be getting cold out here. You guys want to come in for a hot chocolate or something? It's nice and warm by the fireplace. And we can leave you alone to chat if you want."

What is happening right now?

I stare at him, not sure what I'm supposed to say.

The few times my sister ever had a guy drop her off at our place, my dad raged at him, yelling him away from the house in a torrent of threats and abuse. Monica would get so pissed off. And the argument would continue into the house, Mom trying to break it up while I stood at the edge of the room trying to blend into the wallpaper.

"That's uh..." I clear my throat. "Thanks for the offer, sir, but I should probably be getting home soon."

"Okay, no problem." His smile is just like Sienna's—broad and friendly. "Just know you're welcome anytime. And please, call me Al." He lets out a soft chuckle and stands, strolling back into the house singing "Call Me Al" by that dude Paul something, loud enough for us to hear.

"My gosh." Sienna giggles, shaking her head. "He's so embarrassing."

But it's obvious how much she adores him.

Wow.

Who are these people?

This girl is...

I stare at her in wonder, my mouth going dry when she smiles and says again, "So... back to our conversation. Why haven't you asked me out already?"

CHAPTER 7
SIENNA

I can't believe I'm being so bold, but I can't help myself.

If I leave this car without getting an answer, I know I'll spend the whole night lying awake in my bed regretting it. Zander drove me home for a reason, and I really want to make this count.

"I, uh…" He clears his throat, shaking his head like he's trying to wake himself up from a dream. "Was that seriously your dad?"

My shoulders slump as he avoids my question yet again.

Looking back at the house, I try to hide my disappointment and reply with enough cheer. "Yeah, he's pretty cool."

"He's… unreal."

"How so?" I spin back, trying to figure out what he's talking about. "He's just a dad."

"No." Zander shakes his head. "I was waiting for him to rip my head off for keeping his daughter out so late in a cold car. I was waiting for him to yell at me and tell me to never come near you again."

I can't help a punchy laugh. "What? Why would he say that?"

"Because you're his daughter, and I'm some guy who they no doubt think is after your virginity or something. If you *are* a virgin. I don't even know," he mutters before scrunching his face up and running a hand through his hair. "I'm shutting up now."

My snort is embarrassing, so I pinch my nose, trying not to laugh at Zander's ridiculous imaginings. Plus, he just said "virginity" and "virgin," so my insides are flushing with heat.

There's no way I'm telling him what my sex status is right now. We haven't even been on a date yet.

I lick my lips and swallow. "My parents are not the yelling kind. They're very chill, and they already like you." My nose wrinkles. "I kind of already told them about you and how you helped me at the party. You didn't yell at me for puking on you. Olivia told me how you held my hair and carried me up to her bedroom." My expression is turning mushy, I can tell. "I'm pretty sure they like you as much as I do now."

His lips tip up at the side. "You told your parents you got so drunk you puked?"

"Sure." I shrug. "I mean, yeah, it's humiliating. But if you can't tell your parents, who can you tell, right?"

He shakes his head, his brow buckling like I'm trying to confuse him on purpose.

"What?" Now I'm getting confused.

"I would never tell my parents that shit. They would flip out and ground me for a month."

"Oh really?" My eyes bulge. "I've never been grounded."

He blinks, like he can't even comprehend that.

Wow, we're obviously from very different homes. I hope that's not a bad omen. I worry my lip, staring at the dashboard and fidgeting with my opal ring as an awkward silence falls between us.

Crap, what do I say now?

I think we should definitely stop talking about parents.

Maybe I could—

"So..." Zander's voice has that husky quality to it that I know is destined to become my favorite sound.

I glance at him, hope sparkling through me as I softly whisper, "So..."

"If they're chill..." He moves, inching a little closer to me and gliding his finger over the back of my hand. "And they think I'm awesome..." He lightly traces my knuckles. "They'd probably be okay with me asking you out on a date, right?"

Butterflies swarm my chest, their excited wings catching on my rib cage, tickling my heartstrings and causing this bubble of giddy laughter to form in my throat. It takes everything in me to keep it on lockdown.

"Yes." I can barely breathe.

"Cool." His lips rise into that lopsided grin, and my heart flutters wildly, joining the butterflies' rave party, which is moving into my stomach with a raucous energy that's impossible to hide.

A breathy giggle pops out of me. "So... are you gonna ask me on a date or...?"

"That's what I'm trying to do." He laughs, scrubbing a hand down his face. "Shit, I seriously thought I was cooler than this, but you..." His words trail off, and he stares at me through the dim glow of the streetlights.

"I what?"

Holding my breath, I study his expression, my chest expanding when he threads his fingers between mine.

"You're like no other girl I've ever met before." He swallows, then looks up at me with this sweet vulnerability. "Are you free tomorrow night?"

"I don't know, but if I've got anything going on, I'm canceling it."

He grins. "You sure?"

"Yes. One hundred percent positive."

I love that smile he gets after I compliment him. He seems to appreciate my desperation. If that's what it is? Or maybe it's just shameless flirting? Obvious crushing?

Whatever, I can tell he likes it, so I lean forward, then have to clamp my teeth against a giddy giggle when he asks, "Pick you up at four?"

"Four? I thought you were gonna say seven or something."

"Well..." He tips his head, looking playful and adorable at the same time. "I figure we need to go do some fun stuff, and then there's dinner and maybe a movie. And you've gotta have dessert, right? We really need to start at four... or maybe even three?"

I bite my lip, unable to contain my smile. "I like your thinking, Mr. Quarterback."

He winks at me, and my insides melt into a puddle of goo.

It makes it really hard to reply, but somehow I manage to whisper, "Pick me up at three, then." Leaning forward, I brush my lips across his cheek, and before my legs stop working, I get out of the car and do my best to walk to the house looking even mildly cool.

But I'm more like a newborn giraffe, my body wanting to skip and twirl while trying to walk like a model on a catwalk... with the world's wobbliest legs.

I must look like the biggest dork! I'm too afraid to look back in case he's laughing at me or changing his mind about the date.

But when I get to my front door, I can't help myself.

Glancing over my shoulder, I see his car still parked against the curb.

Zander watched me the entire way, and I can tell by the smile on his face that he really liked what he saw.

Holy shit!

Zander Donohue likes me!

CHAPTER 8
ZANDER

The porch light gave me the perfect shot of Sienna just before she disappeared into the house. My heart is still thumping like it only just started working for the first time tonight.

Unbelievable.

That girl is... something else.

A smile tugs at my lips, and they stay that way the entire drive home. Which is like two minutes, because she seriously only lives around the corner from me.

Yes!

I've just had the best night of my life with the sweetest, sexiest, prettiest girl I've ever met.

Listening to her talk about her travels, watching how animated her face was... even in the dim light of the car, I could see the sparkle in her blue eyes.

She's so beautiful. And it seems to be on the inside as much as the outside. She's funny and knows so much about the world. I love how bright her voice is and the way she laughed at my comments, then did that snort thing and held her nose.

How cute was that?

I'm falling already, and we haven't even been on a date yet. This is insane!

My stomach dances and knots as I imagine how tomorrow will play out. The thought of being with her, focusing on just her for a whole afternoon and evening, is nothing but thrilling.

Steering my car into the driveway, I pull up the hand-brake... and my smile disappears.

What the hell is Dad doing here?

It's so fucking tempting to start the engine and disappear, but he's seen me. How long has he been waiting on the porch?

Must be a while. He's looking pissed, even though I'm home five minutes before curfew.

What the fuck is his problem this time?

With a sigh, I shoulder the door open and shuffle toward the front steps. Dad's on his feet and clambering down to meet me halfway.

Before he can even say anything, I go on the defensive. "What? I'm home on time."

"You weren't at Noah's place," he hisses, crossing his arms and looking livid. His large biceps bulge beneath his shirt, and I tense, my fingers curling inside my jacket pockets. "Noah didn't even know *where* you were!"

My insides go cold, my skin bubbling with goose bumps. "Why are you checking up on me?"

"Why are you lying to me!" he bites back.

"I didn't lie. You just *assumed* I was going to Noah's."

"A fair assumption to make!" His arms flick wide. "That's where you always go! But not tonight, right? Instead, you took some blonde who knows where to do who knows what. I swear, Zander, if you get some girl pregnant, I'm gonna—"

"Dad!" I snap. "It wasn't like that. I just gave her a ride home. We sat outside her house *talking*. That's it."

His eyes narrow into fine slits as he obviously tries to figure out if I'm pulling a fast one.

I roll my eyes.

"Who is she?" he growls.

"Her name's Sienna. She's new around here, and I was just trying to be nice."

"Yeah, right. I saw the way her face lit up when you approached the car. Why was she waiting for you?"

"Because I told her to," I grit out, my insides twisting into tight, uncomfortable knots.

"I don't want you getting distracted by some girl."

"Dad—"

"This is an important year for you. You can't lose focus. We want more than one college offering you a place on their team. I want you to have options. Choices. You need to be in peak physical and mental condition. You really don't have time for a girl in your life."

I clench my jaw. I hate that he's taller than me. Broader, stronger. When he looks down on me like this, I feel like a five-year-old kid again, desperately trying to make him happy so he won't get mad and start yelling and throwing things, then slamming doors and disappearing for a few days to cool off.

"I mean, what does she even want with you, anyway?

Is this some status thing? Is she trying to add you to her little black book or something? Earn herself bragging rights because she got to sleep with the quarterback?"

"No!" I bark, fury whipping through me like a hurricane. He doesn't know shit, and I fucking hate his assumptions. But I can't let that show, right?

Stay cool. Stay calm.

My nostrils flare as I cross my arms and grit out, "Dad, come on. Stop turning this into something it's not."

"I've got a bad feeling about it." He shrugs. "I want you to stay away from her. You need to focus on football. That's it."

"Am I still allowed to go to work?" I grumble sarcastically.

"Hey." He snaps his fingers at points at me. "Don't get smart with me. I'm doing you a favor here, kid. You can't lose sight of what's important. Your entire future is riding on this, and I don't want you to fuck it up the way I did."

His words make me flinch, and I glare at him with the darkest look I can muster.

He sighs, his shoulders slumping as he rests his hands on his hips. "You know what I mean."

"Yeah, I'm sure Monica will be stoked to have the fact that she's a big mistake shoved in her face. What the hell is your problem?" My voice starts to rise before I can stop it. "I know what's at stake, okay? You're reminding every two seconds, so it's kind of impossible to forget! I'm not gonna make *your* mistakes, so get the fuck off my back already!"

"Watch your mouth," he growls, grabbing my arm when I try to walk away. "I'm trying to protect you."

I scoff and shake him off me. "Thanks for that, warden," I spit, trying to move past again.

He shifts, getting in my face and making me feel small. His finger presses into my chest, and I'm seconds away from flicking him off me when the front door opens.

"Zander? Baby? What's going...?" Mom's voice trails off as she quickly takes in the scene before her. Her sigh is low and heavy, her voice terse. "Brett, what are you doing here?"

"I needed to talk to Zander."

"At one o'clock in the morning?" Her expression is incredulous. "Shouting away like we don't have neighbors? Honestly. Go home."

"I'm trying to keep our son from screwing up his—"

"Brett." Mom's voice is firm as she crosses her arms and glares at him. "Go. Home."

He huffs, shoving his hands in his pockets and softly growling, "We'll finish this later."

"Can't wait," I mutter.

Dad gives me a stern side-eye before stalking to his car and peeling out of the driveway.

I clomp up the stairs, and Mom wraps her arms around me before I can even close the front door.

"That man," she mutters. "He's impossible."

Despite the fact that I'm riled with my old man, I still find my instincts going on the defensive. I nearly start telling her that he's just trying to look after me, but what the fuck?

It's an automatic response to years of being caught between these two.

Like Pavlov's fucking dogs.

Whatever point Dad's trying to make, Mom's always making the opposite one... whether she agrees with him or not.

"So, I'm guessing he was here wondering why you didn't go to Noah's."

I sigh. "I never said I was going to Noah's."

"I know. We both just assumed... until we saw that blonde girl waiting by your car." Mom smiles. "She's pretty."

"Yeah." I nod, unable to hide my grin. "She's great, Mom."

"That's nice, sweetheart." She palms my cheek. "High school is about having fun, too, you know?"

I bob my head.

"Your father wants you to stay focused, but I want you to make sure you fit in some good times as well. So, you enjoy her company, but... baby..."

The serious look on Mom's face is making my stomach knot all over again.

"Don't fall in love with her, okay? You're too young. You need to keep things light and easy. Nothing serious. You're not even eighteen yet."

"Mom, I'm—"

"I saw the way your face lit up when approached her tonight. You really like this girl. I can tell. So just... take it easy, okay?"

Great, now I'm frowning again.

Mom's smile is glum as she trails her hand down my neck and squeezes my shoulder. "I should have taken my time with your father. If I had, we wouldn't have gotten into the mess we did and then spent years trying to make it work, only to fail. You don't understand yourself when you're a teenager. It's too easy to get caught up in all the emotion and not think clearly."

She's looking at me like she's doing me this huge favor, but it feels like she's just dumped a bucket of cold water all over my epic night.

I step away from her, refusing to give her any kind of verbal agreement. This is bullshit. She thinks I'm going to end up just like her and Dad, but I'm not.

They don't even know Sienna.

Neither do you.

Yes, I do! Well, I'm getting to know her, anyway. Which is why taking her out tomorrow is a really good idea.

I don't care what my parents think. This is my life, isn't it? And they can't put all their shit on me.

"It's late. I'm gonna go to bed," I mumble, kissing Mom lightly on the cheek.

"Okay, sweetie. Sleep well."

She looks all proud of herself, like she's given me this soft lecture that was somehow better than Dad's. But doesn't she get that it's basically the same message?

Stay away from the blonde. She's gonna ruin your life.

Or she's gonna make it pure magic.

I walk into my room, shutting the door behind me and plunking onto my bed just as my phone dings with a text message from my sister, Monica.

Dad wants me to tell you to keep your head in the game.

*Because I value my sanity, I responded with a polite "Will do."
But here is what I really wanted to send him...*

My screen starts filling up with one F-you GIF after another. They get funnier and more obscene, and I'm soon lying back on my bed, cracking up at how awesome my big sister is. I text her with a few GIFs of my own before saying...

Thanks for having my back, sis.

Always. Love you, bro.

I smile, knowing it's true.

Monica might be eight years older than me, but we've always been close. Even after she left for college, we kept in touch with daily Snaps to each other and video calls whenever we needed them. She's never once treated me like her annoying kid brother. And I've adored her since the day I was born. Apparently I used to trail her around the house, and she loved it. I was like her own little puppy.

Damn, I miss her.

Biting the inside of my cheek, I hesitate for only a second before texting her again.

. . .

What do girls like doing on dates?

It takes less than a minute for my phone to start ringing with a video chat.

I grin and swipe my thumb across the screen.

Monica's big brown eyes stare me down. "You're taking out a girl? Tell me everything. Looks. Personality. Meet-cute. I want the full rundown. Go."

With a soft laugh, I update my sister. She already knew about the puking thing. I'd told her about the girl from the party, and she's seriously stoked for me.

"I knew you liked her big. You've been managing to bring her up in every conversation we've had in the last two weeks. You do realize that, right?"

"No." I snicker. "Was I seriously doing that?"

"Yes. And it's taken you a millennium to ask her out. Geez, you're slow."

"Why didn't you tell me to get on with it?"

"I don't know. I didn't want to pressure you."

I smile my appreciation, and we say it all with one look.

Then she grins at me, leaning closer to the screen. "So, this date tomorrow. Are you still in the 'testing the waters, trying to figure out if you really do like her' phase? Or are we going full-blown 'I want to impress the shit out of her'?"

I laugh. "The second one. Definitely the second one."

"Okay." She raises her eyebrows. "You asked for it. Get ready to take notes, dude."

"WE KISSED"

CHAPTER 9
SIENNA

I had no idea what to wear on this date and only changed like five times. In the end, Mom came to my rescue and talked me through a bunch of outfits until we'd put together something that said, "I'm ready for some fun, but I'm not expecting you to spend too much money on me."

"What if he's thinking fancy restaurant?" I worry my lip. "And I'm standing here in jeans and a T-shirt."

"It's a fitted T-shirt, and you have your leather jacket. You look stunning," Mom assures me. "And if he was thinking fancy restaurant, he wouldn't be picking you up at three."

"She's right." Dad walks into the room, munching on an apple. "A three o'clock pickup says *fun times and hot dogs.*"

"Really?" I wrinkle my nose. "I hate hot dogs."

"He's not going to feed you hot dogs." Mom snorts.

"Who doesn't love hot dogs?" Dad stretches his arms wide, his mock incredulity making me giggle. "We did something wrong with her, Bethany." Mom starts laughing too. "I blame the Thai food."

"Or the Indian." She shrugs, getting in on the joke... much to her glee.

"It could have been that goat's milk you fed her in Sardinia. She lived on that stuff for months."

"True fact." Mom turns to wink at me.

Dad's frown is disappointed. "We raised the American right out of her."

"Oh, stop it." I roll my eyes. "I'm *so* American. I love country music, blue jeans, and pickup trucks." I grin. "I love pizza and apple pie and... and football."

"Ha!" Dad laughs. "You only just started liking football, and that has nothing to do with the game and everything to do with the quarterback."

Mom's doing a terrible job of fighting her laughter as she grabs my hands. "He is cute, though, Senny."

"I know, right?" I beam. "So cute."

Cupping my face, she kisses the tip of my nose and lets out an excited squeal. "I'm so happy for you."

"Me, too, kid." Dad wraps his arms around Mom and me, squishing us into a group hug that's making me giggle... until the doorbell rings.

"Oh shit," I squeak, lurching out of the hug.

"Stop." Mom gives me a firm look, but her eyes are beaming as she cups my face again. "You have absolutely nothing to be nervous about. You are a catch, Sienna Beth Erling. Any guy is lucky to go out with you... and don't you forget it."

"Thanks, Mom." I smile back at her, nerves fluttering

through me as Dad answers the door with his usual boom.

"Mr. Quarterback!" He stretches his arms wide as if he's going to hug poor Zander, and I can see the look of panic crossing my date's face.

"Uh, Dad." I move toward them, trying for an interception. If I can just get between them...

"Hello, sir."

"Psssh." Dad swipes his hand through the air. "Call me Al, remember?"

Mom starts humming the tune for "Call Me Al," and I can feel the heat creeping into my cheeks. It's rude to tell your parents to shut up, right?

"Zander." Mom prances forward like an excited pony. Did she just skip up to Zander Donohue?

He's going to think we're the weirdest family *ever*.

"Hello, Mrs. Erling."

"Please, call me Bethany... or Beth. I'll answer to both." She tucks her hair behind her ear, letting out this girlish giggle like she's trying to be fourteen again.

"Mom," I softly plead, grabbing the handbag she's lending me for the night and checking that my wallet and phone are in there. I know Zander invited me out, but I don't want to assume he'll pay for everything. It's such a long date, I'm gonna have to insist that he at least let me pay for dessert or something.

Not that he eats any sugar, according to Olivia.

Oh crap, is he going to buy dessert for just me and then sit there watching me eat it?

That would be so embarrassing and—

"Don't spiral," Dad whispers in my ear before kissing my cheek and giving me a sideways hug.

Meanwhile, Mom is still flirting up a storm with my date.

I move in beside her, giving him an apologetic wince.

His lips curl into the lopsided grin I love so much, and my insides flutter.

"You look amazing," he tells me when Mom finally gives him a second to speak.

Holy shit, he actually means that.

I bite my bottom lip, unable to contain my smile.

Mom swoons, then starts kissing my cheek. "She always looks amazing."

"Mom." I lightly elbow her in an attempt to get her off me.

She gives me one more loud kiss on the cheek, then giggles again.

Oh my gosh, what is up with her?

I send a silent SOS to my date, and he steps forward, clearing his throat and looking between the world's most embarrassing human beings. "I won't keep her out too late."

"Oh, that's okay." Mom brushes her hand through the air. "Sienna can just text us updates if plans change for you guys. Whatever time is fine."

"YOLO!" Dad raises his hands in the air. "Have the best night, you two!"

"Thank you." I can't help a nervous titter as I follow Zander out the door. He rests his hand on my lower back as we walk to the car, and I know my mom's going to be watching and leaning against Dad with a watery smile, patting her chest and swooning about young love.

Zander opens the door for me, and I slip into the passenger seat, waving to my parents, who are still standing in the doorway, jumping and waving like tweens at a BTS concert.

Honestly.

I clear my throat, hoping Zander won't look past my shoulder and see them. Thankfully, he's checking the road before pulling away from my house.

Letting out a soft breath, I relax back into my seat, although I still feel like a ball of nerves.

I'm going on a date with Zander Donohue! Eeeepppp!

Nibbling my lip, I watch him as he flips the blinker and then turns the wheel, heading for I don't even know where. I don't actually care. I just want to be with him. We could spend the night just driving around town and I'd be happy.

"So, are you okay?" I check on him when he hasn't said anything after a whole minute.

"Your parents are like..."

"From another planet?" I snicker, feeling my cheeks heat. "Yeah, I know. They can be a little extra. But I swear, they're really nice and—"

"I love them." He starts to beam. "They're so awesome. I don't know any parent on this planet who would shout 'YOLO' to their daughter as she left on a date with a guy they don't even know." He laughs, shaking his head like he can't believe it.

I grin. "They do know you. I mean, kind of. They know my version of you... and it's a pretty awesome version, so..." A sudden shyness steals the rest of my voice, so I look out the window, feeling the heat flush through my cheeks again.

"My version of you is pretty damn awesome as well, so at least we're even on that score."

I turn back to face him, and he winks at me, making my heart go all soft and squishy.

With a quiet giggle, I lean toward him. "So, Mr. Quarterback, where are you taking me?"

"Well..." He wiggles his eyebrows. "That all depends on which envelope you choose."

"What?"

Pulling to the side of the road, he gives me an excited little grin, reaching over my knees to open the glove box. His hand brushes my thigh, and I feel the current work all the way through me. My breath turns light and raspy when I get a whiff of his cologne, and it's impossible not to close my eyes and inhale that luscious scent.

"Okay, here you go."

My eyes snap open, and I gaze down at the envelopes in his hand. He's fanned them out like playing cards.

"Which one's it going to be first?"

"Oh my gosh, how do I choose?"

"No stress. We're doing all of them, so the only thing this determines is the order."

I grin and murmur, "How cute is this?" before pulling an envelope from the middle. I flip it over and announce, "Number three."

"Excellent choice, milady." His posh accent makes me laugh. With trembling fingers, I wrestle the envelope open and pull out the card inside.

. . .

To win you want to score the least
  The fewer hits the better
  This game can make you laugh or cry
  But there'll always be a winner

"Sorry about the lame poetry." He winces. "It's not really my strong suit."

I giggle. "Are you kidding? I love this!" My voice pitches with enthusiasm because this is so freaking amazing! He made riddles and envelopes for me!

"Do you know what it is?"

"I'm guessing golf, but..." My nose wrinkles. "I'm not very good at it."

He starts the engine back up with a grin. "It's mini golf, and I'm sure you're gonna be great."

Brushing my thumb over the poem, I shake my head. "Just promise me you won't let me win out of pity?"

He glances at me, looking almost surprised that I said that.

"I'm serious." I raise my eyebrows. "That's such a lame way to win. I'd be gutted if I knew you were holding back. If I beat you, it has to be legit."

"You're on, Erling." He nods, his lips twitching with a smile.

Oh, how I am falling for this boy!

"Let's play, Donohue."

CHAPTER 10
ZANDER

So, she's right about golf not being her strong suit.

But it gives me an excuse to stand behind her, wrap my arms around her, and show her the best putting motion and how much power to use.

By the twelfth hole, she's totally getting it, and she actually beats me on the back nine.

"Impressive, Blondie." I shake her hand like any gentleman would do after a sports game.

"Blondie? Really? You can do better than that." She wrinkles her nose, looking all kinds of adorable.

I laugh. "Okay, well, so far I've tried Bright Eyes, Erling, Blondie, and... Blue, which you said I can't use because your dad calls you that."

She nods emphatically, then tucks a long lock of blonde behind her ear.

Tapping my chin, I go for thoughtful, tipping my head and studying her.

She grins, her eyes sparkling like diamonds... and that's when it hits me.

"It's gonna have to be Sparky."

Her laughter is magic, and I wrap my arms around her before I can stop myself. Lifting her off her feet, I give her a quick spin, then grab her hand and walk her back to my car.

"Is it time for the next envelope?"

She sounds so excited, but it takes me a second to answer her, because all I can feel is her body still pressed against mine. It's taking everything in me not to lift her off the ground again and just carry her around like that for the rest of the night.

"Zander?"

"Uh, yeah." I clear my throat, then smile at her. "It's time for your second lame poem of the date."

Her laughter is music. She's living life with a personal soundtrack, and I want to make it mine. I could build a playlist from her delighted squeals, her soft giggles, the little "mmm" she makes when I'm talking, like she's actually hearing what I'm saying and is interested.

Unlocking the car, I pull out the stack of envelopes, leaning against the frame and standing as close to her as I can while she selects the next one.

Her eyes dart to mine, and I can't help glancing at her lush lips before our gazes connect again.

Sparky is the perfect name for her. I swear, her eyes look like pale, glinting sapphires right now.

"Envelope four," she sings. "What's it gonna be?"

She makes a big show of opening it, and I hold my breath, trying to remember what four even is, then grinning when she reads out loud...

"The tooth fairy would kill me for ever suggesting

this. But what's a night on the town without a little sweetness." She laughs. "Dessert?"

I nod.

"Before dinner?"

"Why not?" I shrug.

"I love it!" She wraps her arms around me, and I breathe her in, holding her close for probably a beat too long. But she doesn't seem to mind.

Pulling back, I feel her breath across my cheek as she whispers in my ear. "But I've heard you don't eat sugar."

"That's my dad's rule, not mine. One night off won't kill me."

"But I don't want you to end up feeling sick or anything." Her worried frown is adorable.

I smooth away the lines on her forehead with my thumb. "I'll be fine, Sparks." I nod. "Yeah, I'm really liking Sparks for you."

"Not Sparky?"

"Both work. I'll mix it up, keep you on your toes." I wink at her, and the mushy smile I get back makes me feel like a freaking king. "Come on. I know the perfect spot."

We drive downtown to Monica's favorite dessert place —The Chocolate Lounge.

It's all mood lighting and plush sofas. The cushions are plump, and the music is chill. Bookshelves line the walls, and hot chocolates are served in mugs the size of cereal bowls. The dessert they deliver to us should probably be called Mount Heart Attack.

"Wow." Sienna's eyes bulge as they place the mountain of custard-filled cream puffs in front of us.

The little pastry puffs are covered in streams of thick chocolate sauce and rivers of caramel. Red berries are dotted in the crevices, and white chocolate flakes cover it all like a dusting of snow.

"I see why they call this Mount Divine." She licks her lips and reaches for her spork. "I don't even know how to start this thing."

I eye it up, the designer dessert looking too good to pull apart. But Sienna's eyes are bright with hunger, so I go for it, plucking the cream puff off the top and popping it into my mouth.

The sweet explosion is pretty fucking amazing, but I know after only one that my body will hate me if I push it too hard. I'm so used to my strict diet of protein and veggies that refined sugar like this can give me an instant headache.

I down the glass of water beside me, trying to counter the effect, while Sienna keeps digging into the treat, her cheeks puffing out like a chipmunk, her eyes bright with ecstasy as she moans and licks her lips.

"So good," she keeps groaning. "So, so good." She shoves another cream puff into her mouth, and I study her throat as she swallows it down and feel my insides stir with desire. She's hot, even with chocolate smeared all over her lips.

I want to kiss it off.

I want to do a lot of things with this girl.

Leaning my elbow on the table, I listen to her tell me about some of the desserts she's had around the world.

"And the popsicles with peas frozen into them... they were an experience."

I wrinkle my nose. "Peas? Like the round green balls you have with roast meat and gravy?"

"Those are the ones."

"Where was that again?"

"China."

"Wow." I bulge my eyes and lean back in my seat.

"To each their own, right?" She giggles, licking the back of her spork before finally slumping back in her seat with a groan. "I think that's all I got."

I look at the mound of sugary sweetness and shake my head with a grin. We didn't even finish half of it.

"Can we take the rest to go, though? My parents will love it."

"Sure." I raise my hand to get the waitress's attention, and she takes the dessert away with a knowing smile.

"That's okay, isn't it?" Sienna gives me an uncertain smile. "Or do you want to take it home to your parents?"

I snicker and shake my head. "My dad thinks sugar is evil, and my mom is always on some kind of diet. If I take that home, I'll get lectures on gut health and insulin spikes and how high-performing athletes should treat their bodies like a temple at all times. Blah, blah, blah." I roll my eyes.

"You do have a very nice body." She blushes and looks to the floor. "Just make sure you treat yourself every once in a while. Life is meant to be lived and enjoyed, too, you know?" She tucks her hair behind her ear. "I mean, I get and totally admire the discipline it takes to be a top performer in anything. But I just... well, sometimes I wonder if it's all worth it. I mean, if you seriously *love* football more than anything, then you should give it your..." She tips her head. "I was going to say *all*, but I don't know if I mean that."

I gaze at her, wondering if she even knows where she's going with this. There's something so mesmerizing about her face and her voice and—

"I don't know if there's anything in life you should give your *all* to. Like... where's the balance? Life can't be work all the time. You've got to be able to have fun too. And you definitely should be able to enjoy sweet treats." She winks at me, licking a spot of chocolate off the corner of her mouth.

I watch her tongue move, only just taking in her words.

Balance. Huh.

Yeah. I get it.

Don't work too hard.

Make sure I have fun.

That's what I'm doing right now.

I'm having fun, and...

Shit, I can't even remember when I had this much fun. Since I was old enough to hold a football, the pressure's been on.

But right here, in this moment... I've never felt lighter.

Leaning forward with a smile, I brush my fingers down her arm. "You ready for the next envelope?"

Her eyes sparkle, and it takes everything in me not to kiss her smile.

"You bet I am, Mr. Quarterback."

The rest of the night is filled with arcade games, a movie, pizza on the hood of my car, and finally a game of catch in the park near my house.

It's dark by then, so we play near the streetlights.

I go easy on her, only throwing light passes, but she catches almost all of them, laughing and dancing around between throws. She seems drunk on joy, and I could seriously watch her for... shit, I could watch her for forever.

The lights above us make her hair glow, and I swear if angels were real, she'd be one.

Damn, that is so sappy and romantic. I don't know what the hell is wrong with me, but this girl is...

"Thanks for the best date ever." Our hands swing together as we walk up to her front door.

The compliment makes my chest warm.

"I don't know how you're gonna top it, actually." Her smile is teasing.

"Yeah, well, I had to make the first one epic. I wanted you to think I was the best."

"You are the best."

And there goes that warm feeling in my chest again.

"You could have taken me out to do just one of those things tonight and I would have come home a happy girl."

"Yeah?"

"I like spending time with you." She squeezes my hand. "I don't care what we're doing. You just make me feel..." Her blush is magic, and I stop her, resting my hand on her hip.

"I make you feel what?"

She tips her head back, stretching her arms wide. "Rapturous. Intoxicated. Euphoric."

"And she's a walking thesaurus too." I grin.

"Blame my parents." She giggles. "They're really into the whole 'word of the day' thing."

"I like it."

"I like you," she whispers, her cheeks flushing again. "I hope you don't mind me saying that. I know I can be overly honest sometimes. It can be really problematic, actually."

Leaning in, I rest my hand on the side of her neck and make my intentions all too clear. "I don't mind it so much," I whisper.

It takes all my control to close the space between us slowly.

I want to grab her and press my lips to hers, swipe my tongue into her sweet mouth and taste that luscious, honest tongue of hers.

But I won't be a douche.

So I take it slow, giving her every chance to pull away from me.

She doesn't.

Her eyelids flutter closed just as my lips touch hers. The kiss is soft and sweet, just like she is. I sink into it, enjoying the delicate moan that builds in her throat. Her fingers skim up my arm, coming to rest on my shoulders and lightly gripping my jacket as I thread my arm around her waist and pull her flush against me.

She fits so perfectly.

And I'm starting to experience that euphoria she was talking about.

Shit, I've probably been experiencing it the whole time I've been with her.

But this is next-level.

Her lips are lush and pliant, the pressure perfect. She smells so fucking good, and I want to lift her off her feet again.

This night can't end.

I want it to keep going until sunrise. Who cares about sleep and rejuvenation? I just want to spend more time with her.

Pulling back, her breath whistles over my mouth, her eyes searching mine, then starting to sparkle like diamonds before she leans in again, kissing me with a touch more urgency. I meet her desire, my hand cupping the back of her head as her tongue swipes across my bottom lip.

I open my mouth, deepening the kiss and now making soft moans of my own.

She feels so good.

Her tongue, her lips, her body.

Splaying my hand across her back, I drag it up to her shoulders, then back down and around her waist, lifting her against me.

Her little whimper sends sparks of pleasure dancing through me. Her fingers diving into the back of my hair... yeah, I could get used to this.

I could—

The porch light above us flicks on and off a couple times, and I pull away from her, glancing up at the bulb.

Sienna giggles, resting her forehead against my cheek. "Subtle, Dad."

I let out a soft laugh, brushing my fingers over her ear. "I guess it's time for you to go in."

"Yeah." She beams up at me. "Thanks for the perfect date."

"You're welcome."

"It's my turn next time."

I pause. "Really?"

"Yeah, absolutely. You deserve it."

Damn, she actually means that.

I kiss her once more, just a light peck to say goodbye.

It takes maximum willpower to let her go.

But I do it before that porch light starts flicking again. I don't want to get her in trouble. Although, I'm guessing trouble in her house looks very different from mine. Her parents would probably wrap her in a hug and give her some meaningful conversation. Unlike me, who gets barked up to my room, grounded on a whim, and never given the right of rebuttal.

Glancing over my shoulder, I drink her in one last time, grinning when I see her resting against the door with a dreamy smile on her face. Her eyes are closed, and she looks...

Holy shit, she looks euphoric and... what were those other words again?

Rapturous or something?

I stop, turning to face her and taking as many mental snapshots as I can.

It's not until her eyes flick open that I start to move, walking backward with a triumphant grin on my face.

I can't help it.

She's all flustered at being caught swooning over me, and it's adorable.

"Good night, Sparky."

"Good night, Hot Lips." She giggles and disappears through the door before I can even form a comeback.

She better not start calling me that.

I roll my eyes. Who am I kidding? She can call me whatever the fuck she wants. Just as long as she keeps spending time with me...

As long as she keeps fueling this feeling in my chest that I already know will be highly addictive.

"WE FELL IN LOVE"

CHAPTER 11
SIENNA

It's been five weeks since our first date, and since then, we've been on two more really long ones. It's my turn again next, and I've been trying to think of something cool to do. Mom gave me the idea of paintball last time, and we had so much fun. We even brought Noah, Emily, Olivia, and Kyle with us. Mostly to appease Zander's parents, who seem hell-bent on him not forming any serious attachments with a girl.

Honestly, they act like I'm trying to ruin their son's life.

Zander was stoked, especially because after the game, I stole him away for a trip into town, where I took him to an observatory and we got to see the rings of Saturn through the telescope, then froze our asses off on a picnic blanket outside, staring up at constellations and rewriting myths and legends to give us the endings we wanted. In our version, Hera didn't make Hercules lose his mind and kill his family... and Medusa managed to outwit Athena and turn *her* into a snake-headed monster instead. My favorite rewrite was my version of Icarus, though, where the boy did get too close to the son, but his father managed to reach him in time, catching him before he fell to his death. They then became world-famous inventors, and according to me, the world can thank them for arcade games, popcorn machines, Nerds and Ferris wheels.

"Because who doesn't love a good Ferris wheel ride," I justified. "While eating Nerds, of course."

Zander stuck out his tongue and made a gagging sound.

"What?" I protested.

"Nerds are gross."

I gaped at him. "They're only like the best candy ever. I can't believe you don't like Nerds." I was horrified. They were my go-to and I was shocked that it hadn't come up in conversation already.

"You eat all the Nerds you want, Sparky, just don't share them with me."

"Well, that works out great then." I lifted my chin in the air. "The more Nerds for me the merrier."

Zander chuckled in my ear, wrapping his arms around me to keep us warm. My teeth were starting to chatter, but I didn't care. I would have stayed out under that clear night sky until we were both popsicles. Leaning against Zander's broad chest was the best.

As were piggyback rides to his car, sitting on his knee in the cafeteria, and making out with him under the bleachers between the last bell and football practice starting.

To say he was late a time or ten... well worth it.

That's what he says, anyway.

A week after our stargazing epicness, Zander drove me all the way to City of Rocks National Reserve. It took over two hours to get there, and I didn't mind one little bit. We talked the whole way about everything and nothing.

I also introduced him to Taylor Swift, who really doesn't need an introduction because she's like the best artist in the world, and you'd have to be living in a cave without Wi-Fi to not know who she is.

But Zander didn't really *know*, you know?

So, I played him all my favorite songs, and even though he tried to tell me she was just okay, I could tell he was into her *Reputation* album, and I definitely heard him humming along to "Anti-Hero," which is the best song off her *Midnights* album, in my opinion.

While Tay-Tay gave us the perfect soundtrack for our conversation, I learned that Zander loves watching any kinds of sports on TV, especially the Olympic Games—high jump and pole vaulting are his favorite events. I told him I love gymnastics and diving... and that led us on a tangent of Olympics Games stories. By the time we wrapped that up, we decided we have to attend the games live at some point.

I also found out he's a Broncos fan, which wasn't hard to guess. Plus, he loves Mexican food, and if he's having a cheat day, loaded fries are his go-to. My kinda guy. I *love* loaded fries.

We spent the afternoon walking around that national reserve, then made out against a massive boulder for a while. He's such a good kisser. And I love the way he boxes me in with his arms, his hands on either side of my head, his eyes gazing at me like I'm beautiful. I could have stayed there for the rest of the weekend, his body pressed against mine, his tongue and lips doing insane things to my chest, stirring a yearning low in my belly and heating my body from head to toe.

But then his dad called, and Zander lied to him, saying he was working on an assignment with Noah. He then had to call Noah to cover for him, and I stood there wondering why he wasn't telling the truth.

Was I really that awful?

When I asked, he mumbled something about his dad not getting it and then got kind of quiet and grumpy. We left only twenty minutes later. The drive back was subdued, and I tried to cheer him up by playing "guess that song" off my Spotify playlist. He got into it for a minute, but his enthusiasm quickly waned, so I shifted to movie quotes and then random trivia questions. He did pretty well, and it only confirmed how meant to be we are. The fact that he knew the answers to so many of my questions is simple proof that we like a lot of the same stuff. If only that had been enough to stop him from going quiet and frowning again.

"Hey, Zander?"

"Yeah?"

"You know you can talk to me about anything, right?"

He glanced my way but wouldn't hold my gaze.

"I know you find your dad stressful. Is there anything I can do to help?"

His scoff was sharp with bitterness. "Dad wants my entire life to be about football and nothing else! He won't shut up about college ball and how important it is. It's like he has no faith in me but then expects me to be the best quarterback in the country. Brighton is interested, and so is Kelsey U. Sure, we still haven't had any offers from the other colleges yet, but I've got this! I'll be signing with Brighton as soon as they confirm their offer. I don't actually *want* anywhere else, but Dad seems to think of this as some kind of failure. Like if I'm not being approached by multiple schools, then I'm not working hard enough. But I'm choosing Brighton." He looked at me then, an intense kind of stare before turning back to the road and whispering, "It has to be Brighton."

He raged for a while longer, and I sat there quietly and let him get it all out.

Once he'd simmered down, I wasn't sure what to say, so I pumped Taylor Swift and started belting out the lyrics... and after only two songs, he joined me for the course of "Shake It Off." Epic.

By the time he dropped me home, we were back to laughter and smiles.

I kissed him deeply and promised him more where that came from.

Which is exactly what I'm doing right now.

Everyone at school knows we're a couple, and thankfully, Olivia and her neighbor, Rick, are going through a "back on again" phase, so they invited us out on a double date. To the drive-in movies.

I didn't even know these existed anymore, but we drove about an hour out of Everett to this cool field Olivia had seen on Insta, and here we are, like two couples from the 1950s, making out in our cars while a movie plays on the outdoor screen.

At first I didn't get why Rick wanted to take two cars. It's not much of a double date if we're not hanging out together, right? But from the sounds coming from next door... and the steam fogging up the windows... I get it now.

And I kinda don't mind, because Zander and I are having a great time fogging up our own windows.

His tongue glides against mine, his strong hands roaming my back. I'm wearing his letterman jacket, because I feel naked without it now. I've been walking the halls with that thing swamping me for over a month, and I love it.

About ten minutes ago, he wiggled his fingers beneath it so he could explore my back. I'm glad I'm wearing a fitted shirt, as it makes it easier to feel him. My moan is soft and impossible to hide.

He smiles against my lips, then pulls me onto his lap so I'm straddling him in the passenger seat. I really like the way he feels beneath me. I love being this close to him, and my body is already aching for more. This fire inside me seems to spark a little brighter and hotter every time we make out.

I can't deny this growing sense of wanting more, but I also feel like I'm not quite ready for it. My brain and my heart are at war as Zander's hands keep roaming, gliding down and palming my ass, pushing me against him so I can feel the hard ridge in his pants.

With a soft gasp, I pull back, my chest heaving as I stare down at him.

"My body's on fire," I admit.

"Mine too." His voice is that husky rasp that sends delicious shivers through my belly. I love his voice, his eyes, his smile, his lips.

I gaze at him in the dim light, drinking in his beautiful face—

"Ahhhh." A moan from Rick's car makes my head spin. I glance across and notice it kind of rocking, then spot this gyrating shadow in the passenger seat and—

"Are they doing it?" My eyes bulge.

Zander cranes his neck to take a look and then snickers. "It appears so."

"At the drive-in?" I whisper. "They're actually having sex."

His hands rest on my thighs as a wave of heat crashes through me.

"What if someone walks past their window or something? I mean... I can practically see them doing it."

Cupping my cheek, Zander turns me back to face him. "Don't look. Just focus on me."

I smile, my insides melting as I study his gorgeous face, then run my fingers into his hair. He closes his eyes with a groan, and I give his scalp a massage, nerves firing through me as I work up the courage to ask... "Have you ever done it before?"

His eyes pop open and he stares up at me, licking his lips before shaking his head. "No. You?"

"No." I laugh out the words, because isn't it so freaking obvious?

I feel so clueless on this whole sex thing.

I mean, I guess I know the scientific logistics of it. He puts his thing in my thing, and apparently it feels good.

But that's about all I've got.

I could ask Olivia for deets, but that feels kind of mortifying.

As open as my parents always seem to be, we've never really delved into the whole sex conversation. Sure, I've noticed their flirty smiles and flushed looks when they leave their bedroom sometimes. But no human on the planet wants to think about their parents having sex... and I think I'd rather die than have some raw, honest conversation about it with them.

So far, they've just dropped subtle comments every now and again, like *"Porn isn't the way sex should be."*

Well, I've never watched porn, so I don't know what they're talking about.

"You should save sex for someone who is really important to you."

Well, I've found that someone, so...

"Should we be having sex?" I murmur, then realize I just said that out loud.

Oh shit, what the hell is wrong with me!

My cheeks flame as Zander gives me a soft smile, looking just a touch nervous. "I'd like to. I mean... I'd like you to be my first."

"Really?" My voice goes all soft and wispy.

"Of course. When you're ready, I'm all in."

My giggle is nervous, and I start playing with the ends of my hair. "I don't know if I am yet. I mean... I love kissing you and making out. And sometimes my body feels like it wants to do more, but..."

"It's okay," he whispers, taking my agitated hands and threading our fingers together. "There's no rush."

The look on his face right now... he's the sweetest guy on the planet. "I do want you. I want us to do it..." I nod, realizing how much I mean that. "But... maybe not at a drive-in movie."

He laughs and pulls me down to kiss him. "I agree," he mumbles between kisses, his tongue lashing against mine before he starts trailing kisses down to my neck and murmuring, "There's no pressure, baby. I don't want you to ever feel forced into anything."

I tip my head back, giving him better access to my neck and groaning at the delicious licks of pleasure skimming through my body. A tingling between my legs has me pushing against his hard ridge, and I softly pant, "And what if I'm maybe ready to do more than making out, but I'm not quite ready to go all the way?"

He pulls back, grinning up at me with a level of excitement that's contagious.

I giggle at his playful smile, then enjoy the trembling in my stomach when he tells me, "We can do that."

CHAPTER 12
ZANDER

I haven't been able to stop thinking about Sienna's comments about having sex. The very idea of experiencing that with her was enough to keep me awake half the night, pumping myself dry while I imagined what her body looked like naked, picturing myself sliding between her legs, thrusting and moving.

Damn, I want to know what that feels like.

I've always been curious about sex but have never gone all the way with a girl.

I don't know why. Making out and a little over-the-clothes feel-up is as far as I've taken it. Sure, I've probably wanted to go further, but something has always stopped it. It makes me wonder if the universe has been putting barriers in my way because it wanted me to be with Sienna.

That's probably overly romantic thinking, but I kind of love the idea that she's gonna be my first. I don't know when, but it'll happen…

My fingers lightly trail up her back as she lies against

my side, her soft lips nibbling my neck and sending waves of pleasure through my body.

Her parents went out about ten minutes ago, and as soon as their car pulled out of the driveway, Sienna snatched my wrist and hauled me upstairs. The second her bedroom door clicked shut behind us, we were making out in a frenzy. Her fingers fisted my hair, pulling me close as she moaned into my mouth and we stumbled toward her bed.

I flopped down on my back and she climbed on, lying beside me, her hands sweeping my body as she slid her tongue against mine and made sweet noises that shot liquid fire right down to my dick.

She's so fucking hot.

And she feels so fucking good.

Her boobs are pressed against my chest, her leg curling over my thigh as I swivel to lie flush against her.

Gliding my hand down her back, I palm her ass and can't help pushing her against me. It's instinctive. I need her to feel how hard she makes me.

She tenses and pulls out of the kiss for a second.

I study her face, figuring I could swan dive right into those blue eyes and stay there for... I don't know... ever.

My chest is heaving as I softly pant, "Is this okay?"

"Yes," she whispers, her teeth brushing over her bottom lip before she lets out a shaky breath and dives for my mouth again.

I can't get enough of her tongue, her lips... her whole body.

Squeezing her butt, I then glide my hand up her back

and wriggle my fingers beneath her shirt. Her skin is smooth and perfect, my dick twitching at the contact.

So good. So fucking good.

Splaying my hand across her back, I work my way up to her bra, wondering how bold I'm allowed to be. Will she let me undo it?

She doesn't seem to mind me being here, so I run my fingers around the back of it, feeling the clasp before moving around to her front and lightly cupping her right boob.

Her moan tells me she's into it, so I give it a gentle squeeze and wait for her reaction. Her breath hits my tongue before she pulls away slightly, tipping her head back and giving me better access to the front of her body. I brush my thumb across her nipple and feel the buzz. She jolts and then lets out of a soft laugh.

"You like that?"

"Yeah," she breathes.

So I do it again, triumphant at her pleasure. Seeking out her neck, I trail kisses across her soft skin while squeezing her tits and sending my body into a frenzy.

Her nipples are...

And her boobs are...

I want to touch them without this fabric in the way.

Pulling down on the cotton, I try for better access, fumbling under her shirt until she lurches away from me.

I blink, puffing in surprise and disappointment, as I've obviously taken things too far.

But then her eyes start to sparkle, and she gives me a nervous grin before whipping off her shirt.

"Holy shit," I rasp.

And then she goes and unhooks her bra as well.

Sitting up, I gape at her perfect tits in total awe. They are beautiful, mesmerizing. Those pink nipples and—

"Touch me." Her voice trembles, and I glance at her face to make sure she wants this.

Holy fuck, she really does.

Those eyes. They're bright with desire... hunger.

"But take your shirt off first." She doesn't need to ask me twice. I whip that baby off my body and throw it over my shoulder, my heart pounding.

She drinks me in like I'm the sexiest thing she's ever seen, her teeth grazing her bottom lip and sending my insides into a frenzy.

We reach for each other at the same time, her fingers skimming my pecs while I trace the shape of her tits and feel this overwhelming sense of wonder. It's like I'm exploring sacred ground and...

My thumb caresses her nipple, and she shivers. "That feel good?"

"Yes."

"What if I do this?" With my heart thundering, I lean forward, licking her beaded nipple with the tip of my tongue and enjoying the way her body trembles and shudders. Her gasp is exquisite. And the way she runs her fingers into my hair and pulls me closer, silently asking for more...

Yeah, this girl is everything.

I happily deliver, growing bolder as I explore this new terrain. I suck her nipple into my mouth, twirling my tongue around it before kissing my way to her other boob.

This feels fucking amazing.

Her groans of pleasure are like bolts of electricity, firing through my body, turning my dick to titanium. I didn't think it could get any harder, but it's straining against my pants, aching and begging to get in on the action.

But I told her I wouldn't pressure her, so I fight the pull inside me and focus on her tits. Her glorious, beautiful fun bags... that are so fucking fun.

Smiling against her skin, I work my way back up her neck, squeezing her boob as I slide my tongue back into her mouth. She groans and hooks her leg over mine, grinding her hips against me.

I settle my hand on her leg, fighting the urge to roll her onto her back and just take her.

It'd feel fucking amazing. I know it would.

But she's not ready! So control yourself or fucking pull away!

I can't pull away. She feels too good. I'm pretty sure I want to spend the rest of my life doing this with her.

Lightly sucking her bottom lip, I nibble my way up to her ear and nearly blow on the spot when her hand moves between us and starts rubbing my crotch.

"Is this okay?" She's struggling to speak, and I only just catch the words between her panting breaths.

"Yeah, it's good," I choke out. "It's fucking amazing."

She jerks away from me, her eyes kind of huge as she whispers, "I want to feel it."

"You wanna...?" I glance down and am already nodding.

Her nimble fingers quickly undo my pants, the zipper

sounding loud in the quiet room. Loud like freaking horn blasts heralding the arrival of King Awesome. King Best Time of my Fucking Life!

My stomach trembles when she starts pulling my pants down. I lift my hips, helping her out and feeling kind of exposed as my dick springs into the air.

Her lips part, her eyes rounding when she stares down at it. Her fingers are shaking a little as she reaches for me, wrapping her digits around my pulsing cock.

I let out a groan, my head tipping back, stars scattering my vision.

She trails her fingers up and down my length. "What feels good?"

I can barely answer her question. I'm pretty sure I'm blacking out on uncut pleasure right now. It's pure and raw and—

Answer her, you idiot!

"Um...," I croak. "What you're doing is good."

"Can I make it better?"

"Go up and down," I instruct her, peeking my eyes open and watching her hand pump me. I take her wrist, helping her with the rhythm, then let out a strangled groan at how good it feels.

She watches me, studying my face like I'm some kind of exam she's trying to ace.

"It feels good," I assure her, moaning again when she gives me a little squeeze.

"Have you done this before?"

"Huh?" I look at her, still struggling to think a coherent thought.

"To yourself?"

"You mean, do I Lone Ranger it?"

She giggles. "Yeah."

I let out a choked laugh. "Yeah. Sometimes."

When I think about you. When I imagine doing this kind of thing with you.

"Do you?" I manage to ask.

She shrugs, her cheeks turning pink. "Not really. I mean... I've investigated down there, you know, but..." She shrugs again. "I mean, when you kissed me and squeezed me before..."

I reach for her, squeezing her boob and enjoying her grin.

"Yeah, like that. It just felt... so much better than when I do it."

"I know what you mean," I rasp, drinking in her sweet expression and then closing my eyes with a groan.

"Do you want me to go faster?" She pumps a little harder, and I throw my arm over my eyes, trying to contain myself.

"Do you want me to come?" I croak.

"Yes." Her answer is so immediate that my head pops off the pillow. I blink at her, obviously looking like a stunned idiot, because she giggles at me. "I want to make you feel good."

My tongue darts out the corner of my mouth and I lick the edge, my heart thundering so hard I'm surprised the whole street can't hear it.

"How do I make you come?"

"Just keep doing what you're doing." I glance around her room, checking her nightstand and the desk beneath the window.

"What are you looking for?"

"Unless you want me to mess up your duvet cover, we're gonna need some tissues."

"Oh, of course." She lets me go, reaching over me to grab a box off the floor. Her tits graze my chest, and I nearly bust apart on the spot.

I clench my jaw, hampering the groan and fighting the urge to squirt all over her.

"What else do you need?" Her blue gaze is so sweet, so curious, so...

Brushing my fingers down her cheek, I smile at her, this feeling in my chest so full and overwhelming, I don't even know what to do with it.

"Zander, do you need anything else?"

"Moisturizer," I rasp before I can think better of it.

"Ooo." She gives me an excited grin, jumping off the bed and running into her bathroom. Her tits bounce, and I'm mesmerized by them, unable to pull my eyes away as she runs back toward me.

Nerves skitter through me, anticipation making me lightheaded as I adjust myself on the bed and let out another groan when she squirts a big blob of moisturizer into her hand, then grabs my dick and starts pumping.

Holy shit!

So fucking good. Feels so fucking good!

With a catlike grin, she stretches over me, her tits flattening against my chest as she pumps my cock and kisses my lips. I cup her cheek, my tongue lashing against hers, my heart taking off like a rocket as the sensations inside me—kind of familiar but also new—are amplified by a thousand.

No one's ever touched me this way before, and it's off the charts.

Her fingers are magic.

Her tongue is a spell.

I'm lost. I'm taken. I'm owned.

The moan in my throat grows, the noises I'm making getting deeper, then faster, then...

"Ahhh." I rip my mouth away from hers, tipping my head back and struggling to breathe as she pumps me a little faster, then... "Yes," I rasp, the tendons in my neck straining as this white heat spreads through my body. I've felt it before, but not like this. Not like... "Fuck." I scramble for the tissues, grabbing a bunch and only just managing to catch my cum as my body jerks and releases.

Sienna watches in fascination, the look on her face this mix of wonder and joy.

Her smile is beautiful, her eyes sparkling like pale blue sapphires.

"Wow." She grins as I roll away from her and grab some more tissues. "I've got to admit, I'm feeling like the queen of the world right now. I just made you come." Her giggle is adorable, and I roll back with a smile, grabbing the back of her neck and pulling her down toward me.

"My turn," I murmur against her lips...

Then feel my entire body jolt with panic when the sound of a car pulling into the driveway rips us apart.

CHAPTER 13
SIENNA

"Oh shit!" I scramble off the bed, my eyes bulging. "My parents!"

My hands aren't working properly as I race to put my clothes back on.

Zander is white with panic, pulling up his pants and nearly falling over when he jumps off the bed and wrestles to do them up.

"The tissues," I squeak, my hands shaking so hard I can't even do up my bra.

Zander lunges for them, snatching up the wad and running into my bathroom.

The front door opens, and I whimper, scrambling to put my shirt on.

"Shit," I squeak, whipping it off when I notice it's inside out.

"It's okay," Zander tries to assure me, but it doesn't really work when his voice is quaking that way. He throws his shirt on in one easy move, and I point to my desk.

"Grab my laptop," I instruct him, quickly straightening my duvet cover and jumping onto my bed like I didn't just make my boyfriend come in the most mind-blowing, amazing experience of my life.

Seriously. I want to do that again. And again.

And that whole "my turn" thing... holy shit! Bring that on.

His lips on my boobs before was enough to make me explode. I could feel this sensation building inside my body. It made me tingle between my legs, this pulsing desire driving through me. I want him to touch me down there. I want him to kiss my boobs and explore every inch of my body.

And I want to touch his body and be naked with him and—

"Sienna? Where are you, baby girl?" Dad calls up the stairs.

I close my eyes and swallow, hoping my voice doesn't come out all shaky.

"Just up here watching a movie!" I call as Zander takes a seat beside me, opening the laptop.

Quickly bringing up Netflix, I get a movie going and lean back against Zander's arm just as my mother opens my bedroom door.

"Hey, you two." She beams at us, and I beg my expression to be the picture of innocence.

"Hey, Mom." I glance at her, then quickly back to the screen, pretending like I'm engrossed when really I'm not seeing anything. Seriously, if someone had a gun to my head, I could not tell you what movie I'm watching right now.

Zander's fingers curl around my shoulder. "Hi, Mrs. Erling."

"It's Bethany, remember?" She winks at him, and I look up in time to see him smiling at her. "You guys want any popcorn or anything?"

"No, we're good." I catch Zander's eye. "Unless you want..."

"No, I'm good." He bobs his head. "Thanks, Mrs.—Bethany."

She laughs and shakes her head. "Well, I'll leave you guys to your movie. And I might just..." She opens my door all the way, using my trash can to pin it open. "I'm just gonna..." She points at the big open doorframe and winks again before disappearing.

I let out a relieved sigh, sagging against Zander and fighting the urge to giggle... or whimper? I'm not sure.

My insides are going nuts. From ecstasy to panic, it's like riding a roller coaster.

I feel completely spent.

Zander kisses the top of my head, trailing his hand down my back and pulling me against him. "That was close."

"I thought my heart was going to explode," I mumble into his T-shirt.

He lets out a shaky laugh and rests his cheek against the top of my head. "Tell me about it. Shit, if they'd caught us..." He shakes his head. "What do you think they would have done?"

"I don't know." And I honestly don't. "I'm guessing some long-winded lecture about sex, which sounds really painful to me."

"I think I'd rather die. Like legit."

I giggle and look up at him, lightly kissing his chin. "It's worth the risk, though, right?"

Leaning away, he cups my cheek, staring down at me. "If my parents found out, they'd be super pissed. My dad would probably make me stop seeing you. They don't want me getting serious with a girl. It's all about football, you know?"

His expression gets a little dark, his jaw clenching.

I trace my finger down it, trying to ease that tension. "We don't have to if you—"

"Yeah we do." His face lifts with a smile. "There's no way I'm not doing that with you again."

Relief pulses through me as I grin back at him.

"And next time…" He kisses the tip of my nose. "It'll be your turn to take your pants off."

Heat flares through me, making it impossible to play it cool. My cheeks are no doubt fire-engine red. "Oh yeah?" I'm trying for coy, but who knows what my face is doing.

His eyes light with this affectionate sparkle that I'm pretty sure I could spend the rest of eternity soaking in. Leaning close, he brushes his lips across mine and softly whispers, "I want to make you come, baby."

Rising up to deepen the kiss, I thread my fingers into his hair and love the trill of anticipation that dances through me.

Dating Zander Donohue is the best thing I've ever done. And it's not just because of the searing kisses and this sexual awakening. That's all part of it, I guess, but as his arm curls around my back, drawing me even closer... I know in my soul that this is something special.

I'm falling in love with this guy.

He's no longer just a crush.

He's becoming everything.

CHAPTER 14
ZANDER

Having Sienna for a girlfriend is the best thing ever. At least it would be if my parents and football and school and life didn't keep getting in the way.

It's been two weeks since that heavenly moment in her bedroom, and I have yet to be alone with her again. I'm still getting to see her all the time, which I love. She really is the coolest chick I've ever known. I love her laugh. She has a great laugh, and she gives it out so easily... along with that stunning smile.

She's fun to be around. She has the best stories and the funniest lines. She talks in song lyrics and movie quotes, whispering in my ear in the cafeteria and making me laugh while our friends talk around us.

I love the way she fits on my knee and plays with the ends of my hair. I love the weight of her arm around my shoulders and how perfect her body feels against mine.

I am such a goner.

And I'm happy to be.

She keeps me company with her texts and Snaps

when I'm supposed to be studying or training. She's so funny and adorable. And her honesty makes me smile all the time. Her filter is paper thin—I love that about her.

She leaves me notes in my locker that I read during class. She'll sometimes watch me practice, which is so fucking distracting, but I don't want to tell her to stop. She sits on my knee during lunch break, she sits in my car on the days I drive her home from school... and she sits in my heart—always.

Yes, that sounds fluffy and romantic, but I can't get enough of this girl, which is why it kills me that I've barely been able to find any time in private with her. We make out at school any chance we can get, but it's always stolen kisses between classes or nearly-getting-busted moments in the back corner of the library. She let me feel her up in my car after school the other day, and things were getting pretty hot and heavy—her moan when I ran my hand up her thigh and cupped her between the legs had my dick straining for release. She's the sexiest girl on this planet. I was seconds away from unbuttoning her pants when my phone started persistently ringing. It was my dad, and he wouldn't let up until I'd answered him.

Fuck, it was the most infuriating thing and a total mood killer.

And now it's Sunday, and I'm stuck at home because Monica is bringing my grandparents over for a visit, and Mom thought it'd be a good idea to invite Dad, too, so that we can have a family dinner.

What the actual fuck?

They seriously have no idea how to be a normal divorced couple. I don't even get why her parents would *want* to see my father, but she went ahead and arranged it anyway.

She keeps trying to play the "we're amicable for the sake of our children" card, but it only works half the time.

It's infuriating.

But it's not like I can say anything without making it worse, so I'm keeping my mouth shut and staying up in my room as much as humanly possible.

Sienna's out of town, visiting with some friends who are basically family. I should really be happy about the timing since I can't see her anyway... but I hate that she's out of town.

And I know she feels the same way, because she told me so.

"I do love the Fishers. They're a cool family. Dad was best friends with Keith growing up, so we moved onto their street when we first got to the States. His kids became like my brother and sisters. Russell's a few years older than me. He plays hockey at UCLA and he's coming back for the weekend. So, it'll be nice to see him and the girls, but..." She shrugged, then pouted. "I don't want to leave you."

"It's only for two days." I kissed her, trying to hide my angst and make her feel better. "And I'll make it up to you when you get back." I wiggled my eyebrows, making her giggle—did I mention how much I love the sound of her laughter?

I wasn't sure how I was going to follow through on that promise, but I kissed her deep and long before letting her go. Her panting breaths hit my skin, her voice shaking when she whispered, "I really want to be with you again. You know... like we did in my room."

"Yeah." I cupped the back of her head. "I want that too. We just need to find a space we can go to."

"Something will come up," she assured me. "We'll find a way." Her eyes darted past her house while her fingers curled into my jacket. "When the weather warms up, we've got the treehouse at the back of my place. If no one sees us sneaking up there..." Her smile was electric, and I grinned, kissing her again and willing the winter to be the shortest one on record.

My watch buzzed, and I sighed. "That's Dad hounding me. I better go."

"Good luck for your game tonight. I'll see you when I get back." Her smile was bright, but I could see the disappointment in her eyes.

"Here's a little something for the road, baby." Pulling her forward, I left her with a kiss to remember. It was deep and passionate, our moans of pleasure blending together as heat fired through us. I'm sure her body was as scorching as mine by the time we finally pulled apart —fucking Dad again! One text was never enough.

My watch had buzzed like crazy, Dad actually calling me to demand to know why I hadn't responded to him by the time I pulled away from Sienna's place.

My answers were terse and snappy, and we ended up getting into a big fight before my game that carried on immediately after I left the locker room. He confiscated my phone so I couldn't even text Sienna back, which was enough to make me cold-shoulder him for the rest of the weekend. He was so pissed that he ended up sending me back to Mom's a day early.

Which is where I am right now, up in my room—still phone-less, but at least I have my laptop.

Sienna and I have been texting most of the day, although she's about to board her plane—thank God!—and I'm taking this chance to do some research.

Using an incognito window, I am happily jumping down a rabbit hole entitled *How to make a woman come*. And I'm learning a shit ton of stuff I can't wait to try out on my girlfriend.

There's a soft tap on the door, and then it swings open before I even have a chance to respond. Slapping my laptop shut, I whip around, no doubt looking busted as hell.

Dad frowns at me. "What are you doing?"

"Nothing." I swallow and hold out my hand. "Can I have my phone back now?"

He sighs, stalking into the room. I stay tucked beneath my desk, pretty sure I have a full-blown erection after picturing all the things I want to do to my girl. That last one had me fired up and wanting to meet Sienna at the airport just so I can drive her someplace private and get started.

Slapping the phone into my palm, Dad mutters, "Your mom says I'm not allowed to take it from you again, but I just want to make it clear that I felt it was the right thing to do. You and this girl are getting obsessed with each other, and it's not healthy."

I roll my eyes. *Here we go again.*

"I mean it, Zander. There's more to life than just some girl."

"She's not just *some girl*," I grit out. "She's really important to me."

"Yeah, yeah." Dad brushes his hand through the air. "I get that you're really into her, but you've got a whole future ahead of you. I need you to understand how important that is."

"I get it, Dad!" I huff, running a hand through my hair. This conversation is disintegrating my boner, so it's safe enough for me to push away from my desk and face him properly. "You won't shut up about it, so—"

"I won't shut up because I care about you!" he growls. "There's more to life than romance. How's that gonna help you reach your football goals? How's that gonna get you an education and a job!"

"Dad." I close my eyes with a sigh. "Stop being so dramatic. I can do all of those things and still have a girlfriend."

"She is distracting you, and you know it. Your game-play is off. Your studies are taking a hit."

I balk at him. "That's bullshit! I'm working my ass off on the field and in school."

"Your focus isn't completely there, and I'm worried it's going to kill your chances. Brighton doesn't accept half-ass players. They'll want your full commitment."

"Dad—" I start.

He holds up his hand. "Just shut up for a second and hear me out. I'm not telling you to break up with her, okay? I'm just warning you that if you don't get your head on straight, you might not get the college you're hoping for."

"Oh, come on." I flick my hands out wide. "We already know Brighton's interested."

"You haven't had a definite verbal offer yet, and until you do, you don't have the luxury of relaxing and slacking off!"

"You're being paranoid."

"There are no guarantees in this life," Dad barks, thrusting a hand through his hair and starting to pace. "I was hoping scouts from all over would come and see you, but they won't even know you exist unless you put yourself out there. We should have sent your video out to more schools."

I roll my eyes. "The Brighton coaches have already been to one game this season, and they'll come to at least two more. They're interested in a few of us."

"I know that." Dad spins to face me. "But they won't *stay* interested unless you up your performance! Last week's game was a write-off. Friday night's wasn't much better, and that was a *home* game. You should have dominated."

I grit my teeth and mutter, "That team was brutal. Give me a break."

"You were off your game, Zander." Dad's eyes narrow in on me, and I squirm in my seat, fisting my fingers and tapping my knee. I don't want to admit that he's right.

Can't I just enjoy my life?

Can't I just spend every waking minute with the girl who makes me feel alive?

The thought of leaving her to go away to college

fucking sucks. Which is why I'm secretly glad no other scouts or coaches have come. If I go to Brighton, she'll be close enough to still see all the time.

Which means I only want Brighton.

I'm not going to some school hundreds or thousands of miles away! We can't be that far apart. I won't do it.

"Look, I've spoken to Coach."

"What?" My head springs up, and I gape at my father.

"He's helping me put some more feelers out there, suggesting colleges on the West Coast. Plus, he's hoping the offensive coach from Kelsey U will come to your next game, and he's even—"

"I'm not going to Kelsey U. It's miles away! And screw the West Coast!"

"You may not have a choice!" Dad thunders back. "Besides, Kelsey U is a good school with a great football program."

"No way." I shake my head. "I get that you loved going there, but I'm not you! And I don't want to be that far from home."

"Because of a girl?" Dad sneers.

I clench my jaw and glare at him.

"You can't base life decisions on a girl."

It makes my hackles go up, and I'm about ready to yell him out of my room when he starts going on about how his plans were thwarted because he didn't play it safe. He could have had a football career if he'd kept his head out of the clouds and focused on the game, but instead he—

"I don't want to play it safe!" I cut him off before I have to hear any more of this bullshit. "Just because you and Mom didn't work out doesn't mean every couple who meet in high school can't last. Stop projecting your shit onto me! This is my life!"

"He's just trying to protect you." Mom appears behind Dad, and for once they're actually agreeing on something.

Perfect.

Well, isn't that just fucking perfect.

They fight about *everything*, but when it comes to me and Sienna, they're in complete agreement.

I feel totally ganged up on as I slump back into my desk chair and listen to their lecture on how I'm still so young and don't really know what I want yet.

Screw them!

They don't know fucking shit!

"Hey, family!" My sister's voice travels up to my room from the front door, and I've never been so grateful.

"We'll finish this later." Dad points at me.

"Can't wait," I seethe, brushing past them to run downstairs and greet my sister and grandparents.

Thank God they're staying the night. It'll keep me safe for the next twenty-four hours.

But then they'll leave, and I'll be stuck here with Mom and Dad, who are determined to ruin my life.

CHAPTER 15
SIENNA

Zander has been kinda off this week. I noticed it the second I saw him on Monday morning, but he won't admit that anything's wrong.

He's still sweet and lovely and the best boyfriend ever. But he's distracted. Something is gnawing at him, and I'm desperate to find out what it is. I've tried to subtly prod for information, but we haven't exactly had much alone time together, and he obviously doesn't want to get into it around his friends.

Our usual three-hour video chats that go late into the night have been cut short thanks to his parents... and I'm guessing *that* is the problem.

They so obviously don't want us to be together.

Which is, like... ouch.

It sucks.

I don't know what their problem is.

I thought I was likable. I'm polite and nice to people. Why don't they want me dating their son?

The thought has embedded itself inside me, and

now Zander's not the only one who's kinda off. At lunchtime today, we sat together in the cafeteria, holding hands under the table. Zander's thumb drew little circles over the back of my hand—I love that feeling so much!—but we didn't really talk or look at each other. We listened to Noah tell jokes and laughed when Olivia started hassling him for being a sexist douche.

"Your jokes suck, No-No. Seriously, you're never gonna get a girlfriend."

"Like I'd ever want one," he retorted, and I darted my eyes to Zander, suddenly worrying that maybe *he* didn't want one anymore. Maybe this whole couple thing was getting to be too much for him.

Did he want out?

Were his parents encouraging him to break up with me?

My heart has been bleeding ever since, and I seriously hate my brain for festering on that thought, but I can't seem to stop myself.

I don't want Zander and me to be over!

It makes concentrating in class damn near impossible, and when the teacher tells me off for a second time, I mumble a quick "I'm so sorry, sir. My head's feeling kinda funny." Getting out of my chair, I walk toward him with a big fat lie, leaning in and whispering, "I've got my period, and I'm not feeling too great."

He gives me a quick side-eye and shuffles to his desk, scribbling me a quick hall pass and muttering, "Go see the nurse."

It's an effort to keep my eyebrows from popping up in

surprise. I was just looking for a little leniency for the rest of the class, but okay.

Grabbing my stuff, I head out the door, a little annoyed with myself that I now have to keep up this charade for the rest of the day. Crossing my arms, I shuffle slowly down the hallway, wondering what the longest route is, because the nurse will see right through me and—

"Sienna."

I spin to find Zander chasing after me. "Are you okay?"

He looks so worried, my heart does this funny hiccup in my chest.

"Yeah, I'm just…" I point behind me, then tip my head in confusion. "How did you…?"

"Olivia texted me to say the teacher was sending you to the nurse, but she didn't know what was wrong. I got a pass to come check on you." He holds up the plastic bathroom pass, and I watch it swing off the key ring while biting my lip. "Hey." Zander's voice softens to a gentle lilt as he takes my wrist, tugging me down the corridor. "I'll walk you to the nurse."

"I don't need to go there," I quickly blurt, then squeeze my eyes shut with embarrassment.

"What?" Zander jerks to a stop, his lips toying with one of those smiles that always makes my knees weak. I gaze up at his sculpted face. and my stomach starts jittering. "Sparky, did you lie to get out of class? A good girl like you?"

I can't help a soft snicker, dipping my chin and shrugging. "I was just trying to get out of being told off again."

"You got told off?" Now he's even more surprised, and... well, I must be blushing.

Shit, just tell him already.

I wince. "I was struggling to concentrate, and he kept picking me for answers and I couldn't tell him." I rub my forehead.

"What's the matter?" His voice is all husky, his fingers gentle as he runs them down my ponytail.

"I just... got into my head a bit."

"About what?"

"You and me?" I cringe and bite my lip. "Things have been kinda weird this week, and my brain started spiraling, you know?"

He doesn't say anything, and the look on his face makes dread pool in my stomach.

Oh shit. I'm right!

Just get it over with, Sen.

With my heart sinking down to my knees, I quickly blurt, "Look, if you want to break up with me, you should just do it fast. It'll be brutal, but I think I'd prefer that to you stringing me along and—" My voice starts to wobble and pitch, my throat swelling as I clench my jaw and look away from him.

"Sparky," he whispers, his hands cupping my cheeks and coaxing me to look up at him. "Why the hell would I want to break up with you?"

"Because your parents don't want us together!" My voice pitches desperately.

He snorts and shakes his head. "Like I'd let them stop me."

"But..." I sniff and grab his wrist, brushing my thumb

over his pulse. "You've been off lately, and I can tell there's tension at home for you. Am I the reason why? I've been trying to ask you about it, but I've been too scared to just come out and say it." I huff. "Your parents don't like me, do they? They don't want us together. I mean, I knew they didn't want us getting too serious too fast, but now they're wanting you to end it. Right?"

He sighs, resting his forehead against mine. "It's not about you. I mean... you could be any girl on the planet and they'd be having issues. They don't want me with *anyone*."

"Why?"

"Because it's a distraction." His nostrils flare, and I can feel the anger vibrating off him. "They've been riding me big-time over football, and they're desperate for me to get this letter of intent, but we're still waiting on verbal offers... or written offers. Any offers, really. Until I get one, they won't chill out. They want me to focus on my studies and football and not get distracted by anything else." His face mottles when he lets out another huff. "It's been going on ever since we got together, and I'm so over it. Mom's usually on my side, but she and Dad are double-teaming me on this thing, and it's fucking painful."

"I'm so sorry. I didn't mean to make life difficult for you."

"You don't." He tugs me forward, kissing me like he means it before leaning away and whispering, "You are the best thing in my life right now, and I hate that they're getting in the way of that. I want to be with you, Sen. I want to spend every waking second with you, and it kills me every time they interrupt us or threaten to confiscate my phone like I'm a fucking five-year-old." His voice gets snappy and terse.

I gaze up at him, feeling how torturous this all is. It's unbelievable. He's basically an adult now, and they're treating him like a toddler who needs monitoring 24/7.

"I don't understand why they're acting like this," I murmur.

He sighs. "They're just projecting their shit all over me," he mutters. "They got together in high school, and now they're divorced. They both always go on about how being together held them back and how great their lives would have been if they'd managed to go off and find themselves and not been caught up in a serious relationship. Mom got pregnant while they were in college, and Dad seems to think that's the reason he didn't get drafted into the NFL. He got distracted with baby stuff instead of focusing on the game." His expression buckles.

And my heart sinks, which must show because he leans forward and whispers against my cheek, "That's not going to happen to us. I don't give a shit what they say. I'm not breaking up with you."

"Really?"

"Yes." He's so emphatic, it makes my belly start to flutter again. "And I don't care that they want me to consider colleges that are miles away. I'm not going anywhere but Brighton. I'm not leaving you." His eyebrows rise, and I could drown in his gaze right about now.

He's got the big feels... for me.

My smile grows a mile wide. "I love you."

I didn't mean to just come out and say it like that. But there it is. Three little words that I can't take back. But I mean them with everything I have, so why would I even want to?

I hold my breath, wondering how he'll react.

But his gaze softens, cloaking me like a warm blanket. "I love you, too, Sparky."

Yes!!! I can't believe he just said it so easily!

He loves me!

Reaching up, I curl my arm around his neck and plant my mouth on his.

The hallway is empty, but he still walks us backward until we're tucked behind a locker, our kiss turning into a heated make-out session as he boxes me against the wall and makes me forget everything but his lips and tongue and chiseled body pressing against mine.

He loves me.

Fisting the back of his hair, I softly groan into his mouth, loving the way his hands roam, gliding down my body and lightly squeezing my ass before trailing down my thigh.

His touch ignites me in ways nothing else can, and that burn for him starts to build again.

"I want to feel your skin on mine," I murmur between kisses.

"I know, baby. I've been aching for you."

Pulling away, I gaze up at his face, seeing how much he means it and feeling that warm comfort spread through me. He really doesn't want to break up with me.

Because he loves you!

"I'm sorry I haven't been able to make it work." He

141

winces. "You have no idea how much I've been pining for you."

For some reason, my eyes start to glisten, and oh shit. *Don't cry, don't cry, don't cry.*

He gives me a pained frown. "I'm sorry I didn't tell you what was going on. Shit, I can't believe you thought I wanted to break up with you. Never think that, okay? Not for one second."

"Okay," I whisper, my lips trembling into a relieved smile.

He loves me.

Holy shit, he loves me!

Skimming my fingers down his neck, I fidget with the collar of his jacket, my voice quaking with nerves. "When do you think we can be alone together again? I so wish my parents were out tonight or away."

"My dad's away," he murmurs, his eyes darting right as he obviously formulates a quick plan. "I'm staying with Mom this week, but I could make up some excuse. Noah or Kyle could cover for me, and we could..." His smile grows as he brushes the tip of his nose against mine. "If you wait for me after practice, we could go to his place." His thumb skims over my bottom lip. "We could be all alone together. We could... try some stuff."

My left eyebrow quirks up as a giddy thrill dances through my stomach. "Try some stuff?"

His cheeks flush pink as he fights a grin. "I may or may not have been doing some special research on..." He leans forward, pressing his cheek against mine and whispering in my ear, "How to make you come."

Another thrill races through me—an addictive buzz of electricity that makes my lady parts tingle.

He's been researching?

I have no idea what that means or what it entails, but—

"It's your turn to take your pants off, baby." He crushes his mouth to mine, his tongue swiping between my lips with a hungry possession that I am so here for.

"After school," I pant.

"After school," he mumbles back before devouring me with one more heated kiss.

The bell pulls us apart a few seconds later, and we both jolt, like we're coming out of a trance and didn't even realize we were still on planet Earth.

With a soft laugh, he wipes my glistening lips with his thumb and gives me a heated look, followed by a sexy wink that turns my insides to melted goo.

"I'll see you after practice, Sparks."

"I'll be waiting."

I watch him walk away, my stomach doing somersaults as another shot of electricity buzzes through me.

Yep, I am so in love with Zander Donohue... and he loves me too.

With a drunken spin, I twirl twice before the hall starts filling with bodies and I'm forced to act like a normal person and walk to my next class when all I want to do is float.

CHAPTER 16
ZANDER

So, Coach yelled at my girl.

I wanted to throttle him. All she was doing was sitting in the stands watching our practice. What the hell is wrong with that?

I couldn't stop glancing over to check on her. She'd wave and smile at me, and my stomach would bunch with anticipation. Her, all to myself, at Dad's place. Holy fuck, it was going to be epic.

I couldn't believe I hadn't thought of it before. As soon as he told me he was out of town for the night, I should have been all over that shit. Thank God I chased her down in the hallway.

She loves me.

The thought continues to sit pretty in my chest, even after Coach shouted at me to concentrate, then turned to the stands and started yelling, "You! Young lady! Get out of here! This is a closed practice!"

"What the fuck?" I tried to protest, but that just got me fifteen minutes of up-downs.

Sienna looked like she might cry as she scampered away, and I was about ready to maim the guy when I ran out of the locker room after practice and found her teeth chattering as she waited by my car.

"Shit. Are you okay?" I rub her arms, pulling her against me and trying to warm her up.

"Yeah, I'm good."

"You should have waited in the library."

"I didn't want to miss a second of time with you." She grins up at me, and I kiss the tip of her red nose. It's an ice cube.

"Come on, baby. Let's get you warmed up." I wiggle my eyebrows, and her blue eyes dance the way I love so much.

As soon as I start the engine, I get the heat pumping and direct every vent in Sienna's direction. She rubs her hands together, her teeth still chattering as she struggles to defrost. Shit, she better not get sick. I will be so pissed with Coach if she gets a cold or something. The stands are way more sheltered than the parking lot. She should have been allowed to stay and watch me.

"You ready?" I ask, my stomach starting to jitter again as I reverse out of the parking spot.

"Noah covering for you?"

"Yep. And your parents?"

"They're fine. They think I'm at Olivia's place, and she's agreed to cover for me as long as I tell her everything we get up to." Her nose wrinkles. "Is that okay? If I do?"

I shrug, not really sure how to answer her. Girls love

details, I know that much. With a soft snicker, I nod and murmur, "Just make me sound good."

"That won't be difficult." She winks at me, and my insides turn to putty.

The anticipation in the car starts to build, this excited tension growing with each mile closer to Dad's place. Neither of us can speak, and I have no idea what she's thinking. My brain is running with diagrams and videos of all the ways I can please her. I want to make her orgasm the way she did for me. I want her to feel how epic it is to be touched by someone else that way. To be driven over the edge.

I press a little heavier on the gas as my mind fills with images of her heady moans. Will her limbs shake? Will her back arch? Shit, I can't wait to find out.

The roads have been kind of icy after some heavy snow over the weekend, and as much as I want to speed, I force myself to ease off the gas so we can get there in one piece.

Pulling into Dad's driveway, I cut the engine and swallow before turning to look at my girl.

"You ready?"

Her teeth brush over her bottom lip, her cheeks turning a pretty pink when she starts to grin. "Show me what you've got, Hot Lips."

With a laugh, I shoulder my door open, then run around the car to make sure she doesn't slip on the icy driveway.

We make it into the house, and the second the door shuts behind me, we're all over each other. My bag lands on the floor with a thud while I start stripping off her coat and beanie. The floor is soon littered with our clothing, leaving a trail of fabric down the hallway and into my bedroom. By the time the back of her knees hit my mattress, she's down to her underwear, and my dick is already straining in my boxer briefs.

She takes a seat on my bed and stares at the tent in my pants, her lips parting before she looks up with a heated grin. I let out a groan when her teeth slide over her bottom lip.

"You're so fucking sexy when you do that."

"Really?" Her laughter has a high-pitched, nervy quality to it.

"Yes, really." I lightly push her back, enjoying the view as she crawls backward on the mattress, then beckons me with her finger.

I crawl between her legs, stretching myself above her and gently cupping the side of her head. "Is this okay?"

"Yes," she breathes. "I love the feel of you on top of me. I love your skin on my skin." She arches her back so our stomachs are stuck together, then wraps her fingers around my neck and pulls me down to kiss her.

I happily oblige, sinking into the kiss and getting lost in the heady feel of her tongue caressing mine. Her sweet moans are magic, and her hands painting lines up my back are fucking epic. I can't help grinding into her. It's natural instinct. My body wants to plunge between those legs of hers, but I won't do it. She's not ready, and this isn't about that. It's about me making her come.

Sucking her bottom lip, I nuzzle my way along her jawline, then start to suck and lick her neck. My brain is swirling with all the lessons I've been learning, and I can't wait to apply them all. Inching her bra strap down, I then wrestle the back hooks open and laugh when she throws it away from her, exposing those luscious tits to me.

"Hello, ladies," I murmur, making her giggle before the sound is lost to a throaty groan as I suck her nipple between my lips.

"Oh, that feels good," she squeaks, thrusting her chest toward me when I grab her other boob and knead it.

Her moans are ecstasy itself, and I love that I can make her feel this way. My body is thrumming as I work her tits, then slowly lick a line toward her belly button. Her stomach quivers beneath me, and I glance up. "Is this still okay?"

"Yes," she pants. "Don't stop."

With a wolfish grin, I suck her smooth stomach, leaving a hickey just above her hip bone before grazing my fingers along the top of her panty line. She sits up on her elbows, staring down at me, her bright eyes daring me to go a little further.

Shit, I love that fire in her gaze.

I'm addicted to that spark.

Licking my lips, I gently pull the fabric away, loving that she lifts her hips so easily.

She trusts me.

And I won't let her down.

Throwing her panties over my shoulder, I gaze down at her perfect mound and try to ignore the nerves threatening to devour me. I can do this. I can make her writhe and come and feel that heat spread through her body.

"You good?" I check, my voice sounding deep and rumbly.

"Show me everything you've been researching, baby." She bites her bottom lip again, and I swear I'm done for. This girl owns me right now, and I'm happy to let her.

Sliding off the bed, I settle on my knees, pulling her closer to the edge and gently pushing her legs apart.

She's trembling already, and I haven't even touched her. Placing a soft kiss on her inner thigh, I work my way up, trying to stay attuned to her every sigh and whimper. Trying to remember what the guy was saying about where to place my tongue and what felt good. Closing my eyes, I go with instinct, and the second my tongue flattens against her folds, I know I'm on the money. The moan that rips out of her mouth is perfection.

Wrapping my hand around her leg, I keep going, licking and sucking the way I saw in those diagrams, loving the way her body is responding to me.

Her breaths get pitchy and I take it a step further, sliding my finger into her opening while sucking her clit between my lips.

"Oh shit!" She jerks, pumping against me, her hips thrusting as I explore her warm oasis.

It's so soft and hot in there. I'm in awe of her body, loving the way my touch moves her and makes her writhe.

"I think I'm coming," she groans, and I glance up in time to see her fist her hair, tipping her head back in pure ecstasy as I pump a little harder and suck her clit again. "Yes! Ohhhh, yes!" She's starting to scream the words, and I am fucking loving every second of this.

I curl my finger inside her, splaying my tongue over her clit and giving it another lick just as her body splinters. It's a thing of beauty, watching her back arch, holding her quaking legs as she moans and spasms on the bed.

"Holy shit... Holy shit!" she's whimpering, her chest heaving. I watch those perfect tits bounce, and my erection is so hard it hurts, but fuck if I'm gonna complain about it. This is epic.

I watch her in wonder, grinning as she starts to come down from her high, then blinking in surprise when she shakily whispers, "I'm ready."

"What do you mean?" I run my hands up to her knees, then lightly kiss her kneecap. "You want to go again?"

"No, I'm ready to be your first. I want to go all the way. Like right now." Her voice is high and urgent, the desire pulsing off her basically palpable.

My eyebrows pop high. "You mean, like... now?"

"Yeah."

"I thought you wanted to wait."

"I can't. My body needs you, Zan. I'm on fire for you and want to go all the way. Right now."

Scrambling back up the bed, she waves me forward with urgent hands, and I'm helpless to do anything but push off my pants and show her how ready I am for this.

CHAPTER 17
SIENNA

"You sure?" He checks again before kneeling on the bed between my legs.

"Yes."

And I am sure. That orgasm rocked my world, but my body is begging for more. It's like he only took me halfway, and I need to finish this.

Gazing at his glorious dick, I have a sudden spike of trepidation as I imagine it piercing me, but I want this. I *need* this, and so I shove my uncertainty aside, moving fast enough that I won't change my mind.

Sitting forward, I grab his shoulders and pull him down on top of me. His hard-on rubs against my thigh, and I bite my lip for what feels like the hundredth time this afternoon and smile up at him.

"I want this," I whisper. "Do you?"

"Hell yeah." His breath against my lips is warm and delicious. I can feel his smile when I kiss his luscious mouth, loving his tongue and perfect body. He's so strong and chiseled. So unbelievably sexy.

Splaying my hand along his side, I run my fingers over those hard ridges and feel that potent desire grow even stronger. "I need to do this with you," I whimper. "Like now. I want you now."

"You're sure?"

"Yes!" I practically yell, then stop and blink up at him. "Wait. Are you sure? Do you want this?"

"Yes." He brushes his knuckles down my cheek, his smile so tender my heart feels like it's melting in my chest.

"Then why are you hesitating?"

"I'm just nervous, I guess." A shadow of vulnerability slips across his face. "I've never done this before. I don't want to screw it up."

His expression is adorable, and that familiar buzz of affection I always feel blooms to something powerful and overwhelming.

"I love you," I whisper, my eyes starting to glass for reasons I can't even explain.

Maybe it's the mushy way he's looking at me.

Maybe it's the fact that when he whispers, "I love you too," I know he means it.

Reaching up for his lips again, I brush my tongue against his, and he sinks on top of me. His lips are perfect; his weight on my body is divine. He's hovering on his elbows, but I can still feel him like a perfect blanket, and I want to stay under here for the rest of my life.

As we deepen the kiss, the heat between us builds and starts to spike again. His pecs rubbing against my sensitive nipples sends waves of pleasure coursing through me. Yes, I want this. I really, really want this with a force and urgency that's beyond my control.

And I'm not the only one feeling this way.

My breath catches as he starts to grind against me. My body responds like it's the most natural thing in the world, and I thrust back, my hips seeking him out. His dick pokes me, and he's not quite lined up properly.

"Wait," I squeak and reach between us, parting my folds for him and guiding his dick to my entrance.

A quivering fear travels through me, and for a second, I can't breathe as he locks eyes with me.

"Are you ready?"

"Yes," I whisper.

And he moves his hips in one smooth thrust.

"Ah!" My cry is kind of feral, and I'd probably be embarrassed if I wasn't in so much pain.

"Oh shit, are you okay?"

"Yes," I rasp as I adjust to this foreign presence in my most private place. I feel like he's just ripped me in half, the burning sensation traveling through me a hot fire that's scorching.

Gritting my teeth, I blink at the tears stinging my eyes as Zander lightly squeezes my shoulders.

"What should I do?"

"Just don't move," I whimper.

"I can get out. Should I get out?"

"No."

"I don't want to hurt you. I'm hurting you. I can tell I'm hurting you."

"Just shut up for a second and don't move." I squeeze

my eyes shut. "I want you in here. I do. Just let me adjust to you."

"Okay." He sounds unsure, and I dig my fingers into his shoulders when he seems to want to get off me.

"You're big," I squeak.

"You're tight," he whispers, brushing his lips across my cheek and kissing my tears away. "You feel fucking amazing, Sen."

I blink, pulling my head back so I can look up at his beautiful face. "It doesn't hurt for you?"

"No. I mean, it's a new sensation, you know... but it's not painful." His expression crumples. "I'm sorry it is for you. Maybe I should have just inched in slowly instead of—"

"No, that's okay. It's starting to feel better now."

"Really?" His gaze softens with relief.

"Yeah. I think it was just a shock, you know? I didn't know what to expect, but my body wants you in here, I swear. I just, um..." My breath catches as I drink in his expression. "I love you," I mouth because I don't have a voice right now.

He swipes the last of my tears away with his thumb and lightly pecks my nose.

"I love you too." His husky voice is in play, and my insides tremble with this overwhelming emotion that makes me want to cry for a whole different reason.

I've never felt so connected to another human being before.

Running my hand over his shoulder and down his arm, I notice that he's trembling.

"Are you okay?" Concern flashes through me. "Why are you shaking?"

"I really want to move." He winces. "But I won't until you're ready, okay?"

I nod, licking my lips and finally managing a soft whisper. "I'm ready."

"Yeah?"

"Yeah, just... go slow."

A cute look of concentration crosses his face as he eases back, then slowly moves inside me again. My breath catches and he stops.

"Is that okay?"

"Yeah."

So he does it again, moving with a little more confidence. A warm sensation travels through me, and I can't help a soft smile. This is starting to feel good. When he moves again, I find his rhythm and match it, gently rocking my hips so we meet in the middle.

He groans and I relish the sound, loving the way this is affecting him. Pressing my lip to his shoulder, I do it again, rocking with him and letting out a whimper when this wondrous sensation starts flooding my body.

"You feel good," I manage to whisper.

"So do you," he moans. "So fucking good."

Picking up his pace, he thrusts a couple more times, then starts to grunt and groan.

"Oh fuck. Oh fuck." His voice quakes, his breath kissing my cheek. "I'm coming already. You feel... so... good... I'm—" Another grunt overtakes him, and he jerks on top of me, his butt cheeks clenching as he buries himself, then pulls back and buries himself again.

I cry out along with him, the sensation so new and overwhelming that all I can do is cling to him.

He nuzzles his mouth into the crook of my neck and peppers kisses on my skin before working his way up to my lips. We're both out of breath and reeling. I feel like I could fly.

Sure there was pain, but that finish was...

I shake my head, my smile no doubt the picture of awe and wonderment.

"That was...," I rasp.

"I know." He pulls up on his elbows and gazes down at me. His eyes are so warm with affection, my heart is pulsing with a beat just for him.

I want to tell him I love him again, but is that too much? Too desperate? Too needy? Too—

"I love you." He brushes his lips against mine. "That was epic, and I love you." He starts to laugh, then lifts himself higher and shouts, "That was epic!"

I giggle, running my fingers down his naked chest and loving him with everything.

I'm so grateful he was my first.

I want him to be my last too.

I only ever want his hands on me, his lips, his taste... and I only ever want him inside me.

A thrill buzzes through me as I gaze up at him, reliving our epic encounter and suddenly realizing that—

Oh shit.

We didn't use protection.

CHAPTER 18
ZANDER

Sienna goes stiff beneath me, her expression paling as her eyes bug out.

"Are you okay?" I immediately pull out of her, worried that I'm hurting her again.

Seeing her tears when I entered her nearly killed me, but she begged me to stay, and... and she felt so good.

Shit, I'm such a selfish prick!

"I'm sorry," I mumble, glancing down and blinking at the blood coating my dick.

Reaching for the tissues, I scramble to make this right. How badly did I hurt her?

She seemed to be enjoying it by the end, but was she just pretending?

"Are you hurt?" My voice is frantic as I bunch tissues between her legs and try to fix this.

"No, I'm just... well, maybe a little achy, but..." She pulls the tissues away. "Did I get my period early?" She tips her head back in what looks like relief. "Thank God! I was freaking out that we hadn't used protection."

"Wait, what?" My stomach drops out my ass as the words hit me full force. "Shit! Sen, that's bad. I was too caught up. I didn't even think about it."

"Me too," she whimpers. "I just wanted to be connected to you. You'd made my body buzz, and I needed to feel you moving with me or... I don't know, and I didn't even think about it."

"Shit." I dip my head, feeling like the worst boyfriend ever, especially when she starts blinking at tears.

"I'm just gonna..." She points to my door, bunching more tissues between her legs before waddling out of the room. "Where's the bathroom?"

"Second door on your right." I wince and scrub the back of my head, waiting until she's left the room before lecturing myself. "You're such a jerk. No protection? Seriously, Zander." Snapping my eyes closed, I berate myself for a full minute before finally cleaning myself up and pulling my underwear back on.

Sienna returns a few moments later, still in all her naked glory. She's so beautiful it's hard to breathe sometimes.

I watch her walk toward me, trying not to be a perv. I drink in her tentative expression and feel my frown forming. "What?"

"I don't think it's my period." She rubs her forehead. "I think it might be that hymen thing. I'm sure I've heard about that in health class or something. Girls can bleed their first time."

"Oh yeah." I rub the back of my head, remembering our lesson on consent and then the biology of it all followed by more consent and then... protection.

Fuck, I screwed up so badly.

"What if...?" Her voice trails off, her eyes the size of dinner plates as she stares at me. "Shit, Zan, what if I get pregnant?"

My stomach pitches, and I have to fight a sudden surge of bile that shoots up my throat.

It could happen so easily, right?

My parents are testament to that.

"Fuck, fuck, fuck," I whisper to myself, scrubbing a hand down my face while she pulls her clothes back on. "I'm sorry."

"No, it's not your fault." She clasps her bra, then turns to face me. "I'm sorry too. We're both in this. We both made the choice and got caught up in the moment. But..." She lets out a shaky sigh, hugging herself and looking shit scared.

"Hey." Rising off the bed, I pad toward her, checking her expression before pulling her into my arms. She nestles against my chest, her arms wrapping around me. "It's gonna be okay. No matter what happens, it's you and me together, all right?"

"Yeah." Her voice catches, so I squeeze her a little tighter.

"I love you."

"Love you too."

I close my eyes, resting my chin against her forehead and promising, "I'll get condoms for next time. This will never happen again."

"Okay." Her voice is so tiny it's hard to hear her.

Wincing, I stare at the wall and make myself say, "If there is a next time."

"Uh-huh." She swallows.

Running my hand up her back, I guide her to the bed and encourage her to lie down next to me. We spoon until the sun goes down, not saying anything. She draws invisible pictures on my arms while I hold her tight. She fits perfectly within my embrace. Like we were made to be together.

I try to soak in that knowledge. I don't want our epic first time to be ruined by this stress and worry, but the reality is... we weren't careful. And there's a chance we're going to pay a high price for that.

CHAPTER 19
SIENNA

So, it's safe to say I would have spent the next month freaking out if I hadn't gotten home and researched birth control, then stumbled across Plan B One-Step and berated myself for not thinking of it earlier.

A quick trip to the drugstore and one pill later... and I felt like I could breathe again. Although, I still couldn't shake my worries completely. What if the Plan B didn't work? What if I *was* pregnant?

I spent the weekend forcing bright smiles for my parents and friends, trying to hide my angst. Olivia kept me distracted most of Saturday by dragging me through the mall at breakneck speed and convincing me to buy clothes I wasn't even sure I liked. But I'd been in such a daze.

What if I got pregnant?

The thought was horrifying... terrifying... blinding!

It's made it really hard to interact with Zander. I feel kind of mean for ghosting him. Well, I'm not ghosting him in the sense that if he texts, I'll reply... but I've emotionally cut myself off while this internal freak-out decimates me.

When he calls on Sunday night to check if I'm okay, I can barely talk to him, and he ends up saying goodbye in this morose small voice that makes me feel so bad. But I don't know what to say to him. I mean, I told him about the Plan B thing at school on Friday, and that obviously made him feel better. He was so relieved. So why wasn't I?

It's a total travesty that I should be feeling this way after what we shared together. Sure, it hurt when he first entered me, but the stuff he did with his tongue before that... and after I got over the shock of him first pushing into me, well... it was pretty freaking awesome. And I want to revel in that, not be fighting panic attacks that I'm about to become a mama in my junior year of high school!

I barely sleep on Sunday night and wake up feeling blurry-eyed and incredibly grumpy, until...

I go to the bathroom and find my pajamas bottoms smeared with blood.

"Wait, what?" I gape at my pants, then scramble for some toilet paper and nearly cry with relief when I realize I have my period.

I knew it was due any day now, and I have seriously never been more grateful. Maybe that's what I've been waiting for... without even realizing it. I couldn't believe in Plan B until I had physical proof that I wasn't pregnant.

And I'm not!

I'm so happy I actually burst into tears, right there on the toilet.

Jumping into a hot shower, I let them trickle down my

cheeks, laughing and crying as the hot water washes my body and restores my faith in the universe.

"Thank you," I whisper repeatedly as I dry myself off and step into period mode.

I usually hate my period, but I am loving it today.

"Thank you," I murmur again. "Thank you, thank you, thank you."

Racing through my morning routine, I end up leaving for school early and catching a ride with my Dad.

"No Zander this morning, huh?" Dad gives me a little side-eye after we reverse out of our driveway.

I shake my head, then mutter, "Not sure it'll happen as much now that he has to do his weight training in the morning."

"Why's that?"

I huff and cross my arms. "Because his parents are stupid."

"Sienna Erling." His reprimand is softened by the fact that he's fighting a laugh.

"Well, I'm sorry, but they are. They ride him so hard, Dad!" I flick my hand in the air. "They got this call on Friday afternoon from one of his teachers, complaining that Zander's grades are slipping, and they're on the warpath."

"Yikes."

"And they're not even slipping. It was one test. He didn't even bomb it. He just didn't get his usual high scores, and they're acting like he's not going to be able to graduate. It's so insane. I hate how much pressure they always put on him," I grumble.

"Is that why you've been so grumpy all weekend? Because they won't let you see him?"

A flush of heat travels through my body, and I hug my backpack to my chest. "Uh, yeah. I've missed him."

"Aw. Young love." Dad starts laughing. "It's okay, sweet girl. You can see him today. Just don't be hauling him out of class to make out in the bathroom."

"Dad!" I give him a horrified gasp, and he starts laughing again.

"Oh, you don't do that? So that was just my thing, then?"

"Dad, stop it. Please." My expression buckles. "Gross. I don't want to think about you making out in the bathroom."

His laughter grows louder, and he tortures me the entire way to school, telling me stories about what he and his various girlfriends got up to in the back of the library... and down in the utility closet behind the gym.

Braking outside the school, he gives me a mischievous grin. "Of course, don't you do any of that stuff, okay? You just keep being my good little angel."

I turn to him with a wicked grin. "Thanks for all the ideas, Dad. This trip has been very informative."

He shakes his head with another laugh. "With the amount of squirming you were doing, I'm pretty sure I don't have anything to worry about."

My smile suddenly feels too tight as I lean across to kiss his cheek. "Love you."

"Love you, too, Blue."

I jump out of the car and wave him off, once again flooded with relief that I can joke about this stuff with my dad, because if I didn't have my period right now, I probably would have burst into tears and confessed all.

I couldn't think of anything worse than having to tell my parents I was pregnant. They'd be so disappointed in me... for me. I know they'd support me and everything, but still... I don't want to let them down.

Which is why Zander and I will not be having unprotected sex again.

"I have to tell him." I spin on my heel and run into school, ignoring the curious looks I'm getting as I race down to the gym.

I'm not really supposed to go into the workout room. It's for athletes only, but I check that the coast is clear and am stoked to find the space empty... except for one sexy football player who's pumping iron in the back corner.

He's sweaty, his shirt sticking to his refined body, and I drink him in, admiring his muscles as he finishes two more reps, then sets the bar on its hooks.

"Hey," I whisper, not wanting to scare him.

His head jerks in my direction and he sits up. "Sen. Are you okay?" He looks worried, worn out... cautious.

Guilt rips through me, and I start blubbering before I can stop myself.

"I'm sorry. I've been a really shitty girlfriend this weekend. I know I was distant and hard to talk to. I was just freaking out, you know? And I shouldn't have gone quiet on you. I just didn't know how to deal. And I know it was shitty, and I'm sorry. And I—"

"Sen," he quietly stops me. "It's okay. I was just worried about you."

Oh man, he's the sweetest! My heart is contracting

and expanding for him with these marshmallow beats that make my legs weak.

I stumble across to him, dumping my bag and quickly straddling his lap. Wrapping my arms around his neck, I cling to him, not even caring that he's sweaty and kinda smells. I need to be near this guy.

His arms loop around my waist, and I squeeze him against me, brushing my fingers through his damp hair and murmuring, "I love you."

He squeezes me back, splaying his hand between my shoulder blades. "Thank God. For a second, I thought you'd changed your mind."

I pull back with a gasp. "Of course not! How could I...? No!" I shake my head. "You are the best, and yes, I was freaking out this weekend, but that doesn't change the way I feel about you."

His eyes drink me in. "So, you don't regret what we did on Thursday?"

"No." I grin, then bite my lip and feel the heat rushing to my cheeks.

His hands move to my hips, and he fists the bottom of my winter coat. "Listen, no matter what happens, I'm gonna be here for you, okay? We'll get through this."

"I got my period this morning." The words tumble out of me in a blur, and for a second, I think he hasn't heard me, but then his eyes bulge and he tips his head back with a whoop.

"Yes! Thank fuck for that. I couldn't stop worrying that the Plan B stuff might not work."

I laugh. "I know. Me too. I couldn't get that idea out of my head, and I've never felt so relieved in my life." I rest my forehead against his shoulder while he nuzzles my neck.

"Sparky, I'm so glad. Shit, I'm sorry that you had to go through that freak-out at all, and I promise I will be prepared next time and not act like a mindless asshole."

"You weren't a mindless asshole. We were just too fired up and into it to think straight." I lean back and hold his face, making sure he's looking at me. "We won't let that happen again, okay?"

"Okay." He nods, his Adam's apple bobbing when he swallows. "So... there's gonna be a next time?"

My smile grows as I lean toward his mouth and whisper, "There better be."

I kiss his lips, then quickly deepen it. His moan is delicious as I swipe my tongue against his, then tip my hips and grind against him. I feel his erection grow beneath me, and my body sparks with desire.

His arms wrap around me that much tighter, and I swear I'm contemplating discovering what going down on him will feel like. I want to give him that, but...

His coach walks past and catches us making out. We both get yelled at for a full five minutes while Zander has to stand there with a tent in his pants and my flustered self jiggling on my feet beside him. I hate being told off. It makes my face go bright red, and then I have to pee. It's the weirdest reaction, but I've been like that my entire life. Coach yells loudly, too, and it's a miracle I don't wet my pants right there in front of him.

Despite the fact that Coach threatens detention three times during his tirade, we never actually get one, but we are barked out of the gym, and I don't see Zander again until lunchtime.

As I sit down next to him in the cafeteria, we share a secret smile, and when his hand lands on my knee under the table, I thread my fingers through his and feel this overwhelming sense of comfort.

Everything is right in the world again.

I'm not pregnant.

And I have the sweetest, sexist boyfriend on the planet.

"WE DID IT... A LOT"

CHAPTER 20
ZANDER

It's my birthday, and I'm currently having sex in the sports utility closet behind the workout room. And yes, it's the best birthday present I have ever gotten, ever.

It's been over a month since Sienna and I lost our virginity together, and we've been like horny rabbits ever since. I swear I can't get enough of this girl.

I groan, thrusting into her while she clings to me.

"Shhhh," she reminds me, fisting the back of my shirt as I pump into her hard and fast.

We've never actually done it at school, but the fiery kiss she gave me this morning lit something inside me, and I've been burning for her all day. When she walked into the cafeteria during lunch, she must have read the heated look in my eye, because she beckoned me with her finger and we snuck down here. This section of the school is closed during lunchtimes because there are no coaches or teachers around to monitor the workout room. But that doesn't mean one won't randomly pop down here at any second, which is why we're in the very back corner, hidden in the shadows.

Sienna is perched on the edge of a big storage crate, her panties dangling off her ankle while my jeans are bunched around my knees. Her pussy is warm and hot, and I'm buried balls deep in the best person I know.

Fuck, I love her so much.

She whimpers against my skin, her lips trailing kisses up to my ear as I close my eyes and grunt, grabbing her ass cheeks and pumping into her a little harder. It's like I can't get close enough. I wish we were naked. I wish I could have spent the afternoon exploring her body and making her come.

Instead, I'd quickly fingered her, rubbing her clit the way I know she likes and making her body vibrate while she bit back her whimpers and rolled a condom over my dick.

"Baby," she mewls in my ear.

It sounds almost like a cry, and for a second, I worry that I'm going too hard. Am I hurting her? She's so addictive, it's easy to get caught up and lost within her.

I nearly stop to check, but then she groans, "I love you, baby," before sucking my neck. Another moan builds in her throat, and then she lets out this sweet gasp. I know that sound. I love that sound. I'm making her come again.

The thought has me thrusting that much faster, and then I'm coming in a rush of my own, that addictive thrill spreading through me as I jerk and plunge deep, lifting her off the crate and holding her tight against me as we shudder and moan in unison.

"I can't get enough of you," I mumble against her lips.

She giggles. "I can't get enough of you either." Her tongue owns me, gliding into my mouth with a languid kiss that turns my insides to jelly. "And there's more coming after school, birthday boy." She leans back and wiggles her eyebrows.

"Is sex my only present for my birthday? Because I am seriously okay with that."

She laughs. "Of course not." Her legs squeeze my waist as she kisses me deep again, distracting me from the outside world.

Until the bell rings.

"Shit." I pull away from her with a groan, lifting her off me and placing her back on her feet.

"Eep." She scrambles for her bag, yanking out a tissue and holding one between her legs.

I take the one she passes me with a soft laugh and roll the condom off, wrapping it up and fisting it in my hand. "That was hot, Sparks."

"I know, right?" Her eyes dance and sparkle the way I love so much. "That thrill of getting caught really adds an edge." Pulling her panties back on, she adjusts herself, then wraps her arms around me. "Although, my heart is pounding so hard right now. I'm not sure I could handle this on the regular."

Gazing at her with all the affection pulsing through me, I drink in her gorgeous face and kiss her one last time before taking her hand and forcing us back to class. We make it out of the workout room and gym without getting busted and then have to start running.

If I'm late to class again, I'm gonna get a detention,

and Dad will kill me. He's turned into a freaking drill sergeant around me lately, and it's fucking painful.

"I'll see you after class," Sienna purrs just before I leave her. "You can get the rest of your gift then." She bites her bottom lip, sending my body into a whole new frenzy.

Gripping her hand before she can let me go, I pull her back against me. "You know, we could just bail now."

She giggles. "And get you into even more trouble? Forget it. I've got it all planned. Trust me. It's going to be epic." And there go her eyebrows again, wiggling away and setting my body on fire.

She slips away from me, and I run to Biology, getting there in the nick of time.

"You're twenty seconds away from a detention, Mr. Donohue," the teacher warns as I take a seat at the back and smirk at Kyle... who knows exactly what I've been up to.

"You can thank *me* for that, man. I'm the one who told her about the utility closet."

"Really?" We fist-bump, and I grin at him. "I will be forever in your debt, bro. Thank you." My smile grows. "Like seriously... *thank you.*"

"Happy birthday, dude." He laughs, rolling his eyes and shaking his head, but like he can talk. He's hooked up with Georgia now, and those two are as bad and Sen and me.

Or maybe not.

We've been doing it a lot since her period finished.

It takes a lot of sneaking around, but we're making it work. I'm pretty sure the universe is on our side, because we have yet to be caught, and the one other time we accidentally forgot protection, I pulled out and came on her stomach, so we're covered. She got her period last weekend, and that's just more proof as far as I'm concerned.

As soon as Sienna's period was done that first time, we were all over each other. We took it easy at first. I didn't want to hurt her again, and although I think I probably did, she kept telling me it was worth it. Her body has completely adjusted to mine now, and we've even started trying different positions and stuff. It's freaking epic. I love my girl, and getting to be with her that way is mind-blowing. She's so sexy and sweet and willing to try shit.

I love her curiosity.

Her trust.

Her honesty.

Turns out she's not afraid to tell me what she does and doesn't like. I'm getting to know the spots that make her moan the loudest and exactly what I need to do with my tongue and fingers. Damn, it's fire.

She keeps asking me what works for me, but I'm pretty much an "anything" kinda guy. Because just her sweet smell can get me going. Her touch on any part of my body is heaven. And being inside her... it's the best feeling in the whole fucking world. I love the way she'll stare up at me, smile at me, tell me she loves me.

The girl adores me, and that's a pretty fucking phenomenal feeling.

Better than the vibes I'm getting from everyone else in my life. My dad seems to be permanently pissed no matter what I do. The fact that we got eliminated from the playoffs after round one hasn't helped much. Even I was bummed out about that, but then Sienna was waiting for me after the game and made it all better.

And now that football season is over, I've got a little more time on my hands, and it's made being with my girl that much easier.

Dad just needs to chill out. So I'm an hour later for dinner every now and then. He treats it like a fucking crime against humanity. And my mom's jumping on board with all the bullshit, putting curfews on me, which I've never had before.

It's like they missed the memo that the football season is over. They're still riding me about workouts and conditioning and study. They won't shut the fuck up about college and have already started freaking out that no letter of intent is coming. Why can't they have a little faith in me? It's Brighton or nothing. I don't need to be hitting up a bunch of other schools. Coach Watkins from Brighton thinks I'm great. He told me so last year, and he's been to three games this season. He made it clear last time we spoke that I was his first pick, and come signing day, I'll be scribbling my name on a piece of paper with a Brighton College letterhead.

Why the fuck do they keep doubting that's gonna happen?

I'm sick of everybody ragging on me. My teachers have even joined the party, telling me I'm not focused enough in class, warning me that my work isn't up to standard.

What the hell?

I'm doing it, aren't I?

I'm handing that shit in like they want me to.

I don't know what the hell everyone's problem is.

The only bright spot in every day is Sienna. As soon as I wake up, I'm texting her... or if I'm lucky, I wake up with her in my arms. The only sucky thing about that is having to set the alarm for four in the morning so I can get back home in time and no one will know what we've been up to. But I love sleeping beside her. I love falling asleep together, whispering to her under the covers, talking about how epic our life is going to be and how awesome it'll be when we can get our own place.

Once she graduates from high school, she's going to join me at Brighton, and then after college, we're going to travel for a while the way her parents did before coming back here to settle down. We're not sure what state we want to live in yet, but there's plenty of time to work out all those details.

For now, we're having fun thinking about prom and my graduation, dreaming about what we'll get up to over the summer. We have enough plans to keep us busy until her first day back at school... and my first day of college.

I love mapping out my life with her.

I love the way we seem to see everything the same way... be on the same page.

"Mr. Donohue!" The teacher snaps me back to the present, and I jerk up in my seat and then have to suffer a lengthy lecture on how important the rest of my year is and how I shouldn't be wasting it daydreaming.

The students around me snicker while I shift uncomfortably in my seat and start counting down the minutes until I get to be with Sienna again.

Time drags on at a snail's pace, my last class before

PE mind-numbingly boring. Now I just have to get through basketball skills and the final bell will serenade my freedom.

I dribble the ball, my shoes squeaking on the gym floor as we run through the drills our PE teacher is making us do.

Sweat is dribbling down the back of my neck, and I swipe some off my forehead before passing the ball to Jamie. He catches it and does a spin, throwing it toward the hoop for a sweet three-pointer. Too bad we're not playing an actual game.

I clap my hands and run back to position, eyeing the door to the workout room and getting distracted by memories of being in the utility closet with Sienna. Damn, that was so freaking hot.

"Heads up!"

A ball comes firing toward me, and I only just dodge it.

"Focus, Donohue!" Mr. Henley yells at me while I sheepishly run after the ball, gathering it up and dribbling it back to half court.

Glancing at the clock, I thank God there's only five minutes left before firing a shot at the hoop and totally missing it.

My teacher groans behind me, mumbling a bunch of expletives he thinks we can't hear while I ignore his foul mood and focus on the fact that it's my fucking birthday, and I'm gonna be spending it with my girlfriend.

CHAPTER 21
SIENNA

"Happy birthday again!" I squeal, jumping into Zander's arms when he runs out of the gym and straight toward me. I wrap my legs around his waist and kiss that sweaty face of his. He didn't even bother showering, but he still smells good. "Mmmmm." I cling to him. "Delicious. Why do you always smell so good? Even when you haven't showered."

"Shower in a can, baby."

I laugh and squeal again when he starts running for his car with me still in his arms.

"So, how are we celebrating the rest of my birthday?" He pops me on the ground before opening the passenger door for me. I slip into his car and feel that surge of energy buzz through me again.

I've been planning his surprise for weeks, saving up my pennies and scheming with my friends. Thankfully, all of them get how in love we are and are happy to give me this massively huge assist. I owe them big-time, and

I'm taking a whole heap of risks, but I just really want Zander to have a birthday without any adult pressure.

No arguments.

No put-downs.

No you-should-be-doing-betters.

I just want him to have fun.

Which is why when he pulls out of his parking space, I direct him toward the highway.

"The highway?" He grins at me. "You taking me out of town, baby?"

"Yes. I'm kidnapping you for the night."

He pauses at the school exit and gapes at me for a second.

I giggle and can't help telling him everything on the spot. "Your parents think you're at Noah's house for a birthday sleepover with Kyle. He managed to convince them that your traditional family birthday dinner can be postponed until Saturday... which Monica was happy to go along with." I wink at him. Yes, I adore his sister and love the fact that she was all over this with me. "She's totally helped me sell that to your mom. Noah worked on your dad, and Olivia is covering for me with my parents. They think we're taking you out to dinner, and then I'm spending the night with Olivia while you hang with Noah. It's all sorted, babe."

His eyes fill with that gooey look I love, and I lean over to peck his lips.

"You're so amazing." He grins, pulling away from the school.

"Thank you." I can't help a proud smirk as I place my feet on the dash, then start singing along to the music.

He joins me, and we sing and laugh and talk about our favorite birthdays over the years while we drive to a little Airbnb cabin I secured thanks to Monica. It's in the woods, and the pictures were so gorgeous. It looks idyllic, and I just know this will be the perfect night.

It takes us about two hours to get there, and as we wind our way down the long driveway, it feels like we're leaving this world and escaping into a private oasis where no one can reach us.

"Oh wow." Zander parks outside the cute little log cabin.

I do a happy dance in the passenger seat, clapping my hands before jumping out of the car. "This is so perfect!"

"You're perfect." Zander grins across the top of the car, and I run around, jumping into his arms.

I love the way he catches me so easily.

I love how strong he is.

I love the way his tongue feels, gliding into my mouth and setting my body on fire all over again.

He starts carrying me toward the stairs, still kissing me, cupping the back of my head and inhaling me like I'm his favorite food.

I am so here for this!

"Where's the key?" he murmurs between kisses.

"Let me just"—I swipe my tongue against his—"check my"—I suck his bottom lip—"phone."

Easing back, he puts me down and lets me check my phone.

"Can you grab the bag out of the trunk?"

"Yes, ma'am." He runs back to grab the stuff I secretly packed for us. The clothes actually belong to Noah, and I bought Zander a new toothbrush so I didn't spoil the surprise. I would have snuck into his house, but sadly his parents don't like me very much, although Zander assures me that they wouldn't like *any* girl and it's not personal against me. It's hard to believe sometimes, but I appreciate him trying to make me feel better about it all.

"They just don't think I'm ready for a relationship. I should be focusing on school," he grumbled last time we talked about it.

They're so full of shit. They seriously need to get over themselves. Zander and I are perfect together, and one day, they're going to realize that.

I read through my email and follow the instructions the owner left me. Punching in the lockbox code, I pull out the key and ceremoniously unlock the door.

Zander grins, sweeping me into his arms and carrying me across the threshold. I giggle and swoon when he spins me around and then walks me straight into the bedroom.

"This place is sick." He looks around in awe, and I feel like a queen.

Yes, I did well.

"Happy birthday, baby."

He smiles at me, brushing his lips across my nose before dropping me onto the bed. "I think I'm gonna like playing house with you."

Shedding his jacket, he gives me an appreciative look, his eyes trailing down my body as I lie on the bed. Biting my bottom lip, I give him my best bedroom eyes and softly say, "Do you want to unwrap your present now?"

I point to myself, and his eyes light with desire as he pounces toward me with a playful growl.

I squeal and catch him against me, loving his weight as he covers my body, devouring me with hungry kisses.

"Wait, wait, wait." I slow him down, panting between searing lip-locks.

He moves off me and looks mildly confused as I unzip my jacket, then tease the bottom of my shirt. "There's something a little extra here for you."

"Extra?" He laughs. "Your naked body is under there. I don't need more than that."

Aw. He says the sweetest things!

"Come on," I encourage him, lifting the bottom of my shirt.

He does as I ask, slowly slipping my jacket off and then pulling the shirt over my head. As soon as he spots the festival tickets taped to my stomach he starts to laugh.

"What's this?" Carefully detaching the printed pages, he reads them over, then lets out a whoop. "Are you serious?"

"Yes." I giggle. "Three of your favorite bands are playing at it. I had to get you tickets, babe. And I'm really hoping you'll take me."

"Of course I'm taking you." He dives for my lips again, kissing me like it's the only thing he was made for. "You are the best girlfriend in the whole fucking world!"

I laugh against his lips.

Leaning back, he cups my cheek and gives me his "I love you" smile. "This is the best birthday I've ever had."

"And the night's only just beginning."

CHAPTER 22
ZANDER

This girl is unbelievable.

She did all of this... for me.

No one's ever gone to so much effort, and I don't know if I can express how much it means to me.

So I kiss her... and slowly undress her... then worship her luscious body, telling her how much I love every curve and crevice.

I lick her pussy until she's whimpering. I push my fingers inside her, making her come in a hot, wet rush before carrying her to the shower. We kiss under the spray and soap each other down. She makes me fire off against the tiles, working my cock with her sudsy fingers. The groans coming out of me were so embarrassing, but she looked triumphant as my body jerked and released.

It was the best shower ever.

I'm having a lot of bests today.

Once we're wrapped up in pajamas and I've built a fire, we snuggle in front of it, munching on all my favorite snacks. She keeps trying to sneak Nerds into my bowl of popcorn, but I catch her out every time and we soon get into a popcorn fight that leads to a sexy tussle on the floor. After a searing hot make out session, we act like two drunk, giggly idiots, cleaning up our popcorn mess while playing "guess the movie quote" and then starting to dream again. As she curls against me on the tidy floor, we talking about the different trails we want to hike around the world and some of the places we want to see. She's seen so much already, but she wants to revisit them all... with me.

She makes me feel so important. So good about everything.

I matter to this girl.

She's everything.

Spearing a marshmallow, I hold it over the embers of the fire and roast it for her. I have no idea how much money she must have spent on all this food and this cozy log cabin.

"It's your eighteenth birthday. I had to make it extra special," she said when I commented on it.

I feed her the marshmallow, laughing when the sticky sweetness sticks to her chin.

"Here, let me." Sucking it off her smooth skin, I keep going, working my way down her body.

Her moans override the soft music playing behind us, and I start undressing my girl in front of the fire.

"You warm enough?"

"Yes," she whispers, her eyes closing, her head tilting back as I suck her nipple into my mouth.

"I love your tits. Have I told you how much I love your tits?"

188

She giggles. "Yes, baby. And they love you too."

My lips make a soft pop as I suck her again, then draw my mouth away. Leaning back, I drink her in, gazing down at her luscious body, then slowly pull her pajama pants off. My fingers skim her stomach before inching down to her sweet spot.

Her groan is smooth and languid, her head tipping back as I work her clit. Her blonde locks tumble over her shoulder, and they seem to glimmer in the firelight as she heaves and groans beneath me.

Leaning back over her, I start kissing her tits again, my tongue swirling around her nipple while my fingers explore her warm oasis.

"Yes," she moans, her soft pants making my dick hard and eager.

"You're so wet, Sparky."

"You make me wet... and needy." She gasps. "So... oh... shiiiiit." The word drags out of her mouth as I work my fingers a little harder and she starts to come all over them.

"That's it, baby. Come for me."

Her head tips back, her groans of pleasure filling the cabin as she arches her hips and rides my fingers. Leaning forward, I take the chance to suck her clit between my lips, and she practically takes off.

Her cries are the sexiest thing I've ever heard, and when she slowly sinks back to the floor, I swear I've never loved her more.

"Baby," she whimpers, pushing my shoulders and forcing me back.

Flopping onto the floor with a laugh, I enjoy the show

as she roughly pulls off my pants. My dick springs to attention, and she gives it a long, sexy lick before crawling up my body. Reaching behind me, I scramble for a condom. She brought an entire box, and I gleefully yank one out, my hands shaking as she slides my dick between her boobs and threatens to make me come on the spot.

Her tongue starts painting my torso, and then she straddles me, her wet heat dripping over my cock.

"Fuck, Sen. You're so hot."

"Only for you." She winks at me, snatching the condom out of my hand and ripping the packet open with her teeth.

I groan, watching her with hungry eyes as I rest my hands on her thighs and give them a light squeeze.

As soon as I'm sheathed, she hovers over me, lifting my dick and lining us up. She sinks onto me with a pleasant moan that rockets right through me.

She feels so fucking good, I'm seeing stars already.

My fingers dig into her hips as she starts to ride me in the firelight. The flames flicker, creating an ethereal glow over her naked skin, and I am undone.

"Feels so good, baby." She rests her hands on my chest, rocking over me, her wet core sending my body into a frenzy.

I grunt and clench my jaw, trying to hold out and make it last.

She's so hot right now, I want to pop right off. But I don't want to shortchange her either. The little pants coming out of her are sexy as hell, and I want them to last. Sitting up, I change position, drawing this out for as long as my body will let me.

Her boobs bounce against my chest, and I kiss the tops of them, licking between them, then up to her collarbone as she grips my shoulders and rides me like a queen.

I can't hold out much longer.

She feels too good.

She's too... too...

"Ah!" I groan, my body firing rockets as I jerk beneath her, thrusting up hard and fast, clutching her butt cheeks and holding her onto me.

Wrapping her arms around me, she squeezes my shoulders and lightly bites my neck, her teeth scraping over my skin before she sucks the spot, no doubt leaving a decent hickey behind.

I'll take it. I want her mark on me.

I want the whole fucking world to know she's my girl.

I'm obsessed with her, and I don't want to do anything but be by her side.

As the night wears on, we eventually climb into bed, snuggling our naked bodies together and drifting off to sleep.

This day has been perfect.

This night is one I'll remember forever.

But the phone call that wakes us the next morning... yeah, that's something I want to forget.

CHAPTER 23
SIENNA

A phone is incessantly ringing, and I can't figure out why. Squeezing my eyes shut with a moan, a slow smile forms on my face when I register the strong arm wrapped around my body. Zander's hand is tucked under my right boob as he spoons me from behind.

We're both naked, and I'm pretty sure this is what paradise feels like.

If paradise can be a feeling, which surely it is because I am reveling in it.

The phone starts up again, and I groan.

"Is that yours?" I mumble.

"Yeah, I'm trying to ignore it." His lips brush the back of my neck and I burrow into him, smirking when his erection digs into my butt.

That might be a nice way to start the day.

Although, my body is kind of aching from all the lovemaking throughout the night, but it might be worth it. I'll just ask him to be gentle, take it slow. Just a nice, easy ride into consciousness.

I'm seconds away from reaching behind me and making this happen when the phone starts ringing *again*.

"Shit!" Zander barks. "Leave us the fuck alone." Throwing the covers back, he stalks over to his bag, grumbling about how he should have turned the damn thing off. "Noah, this better be good!" he growls... then jerks to a stop and goes deathly pale.

I bolt up, instantly worried... and rightfully so.

"Dad," he chokes out. "What's up? Why do you... why do you have Noah's phone?"

"Because I'm standing in his bedroom looking for my son who is supposed to be here!" He yells the words so loud that even I can hear him.

I wince, sudden tears burning me eyes as I see my awesome plan going up in smoke.

Shit. Zander is going to get in so much trouble for this.

He plunks down onto the edge of the bed, and I scramble over to him, leaning my ear close to his face so I can hear what his dad is saying.

"Now, Noah won't tell me where the hell you are. He doesn't know, *apparently*." The scorn in his father's voice makes my insides shudder. I can only imagine what Noah is going through right now. The poor guy is probably standing there in boxer shorts—or whatever he wears to bed—and shuffling on his feet with an anxious frown. I can picture the scene so clearly. "You listen to me, son. You get your ass back here right now!"

"Dad, I—"

"No! Zander, no! No excuses. I know you're with that little girlfriend of yours. I know you spent the night together, and I'm not stupid. I know exactly what you got up to."

My eyes are burning in earnest now, and I'm seconds away from crying.

Shit, shit, shit! This is so bad.

"Get back here, do you understand me? You pack your stuff, and you drive back to your mother's house right now! We'll be waiting for you there."

"Dad... no." Zander's voice is trembling, and I really admire the way he's trying to fight, but it's so obviously a losing battle. "This is my birthday present, and we're not due back until—"

"I don't give a fuck what this is!" his dad barks. "You shouldn't be doing it. You've only just turned eighteen, and you're too young. I don't care what you think, but it's the truth. You're too young, Zander. And I won't let you fuck up your future. Now, you get home right now. I've just had a very important phone call from Coach Jones at Kelsey U. We need to talk about this, because your future depends on it."

"What do you mean?" Zander goes still, his eyes bulging.

"It means Brighton might not be your best option anymore." His dad sighs. "I'm sorry, son."

"What?"

"Just get home so we can talk about it, okay?" His dad's voice is all soft now, like he's sad or something.

I frown and try to catch Zander's eye, but he won't look at me. His gaze is trained on the floor, his breath on hold until he huffs out, "Dad, what's going on?"

"Brighton might say they want you... but you're not

the only quarterback they're interested in, and I don't think you want to be riding the bench for an entire season. Now, get your ass home. This is important." His dad's tone sharpens to terse again, and I wince.

Fisting the sheet against my body, I watch Zander's head bob up and down as he shifts toward his gear bag. "Yeah, I'm on my way." His voice trembles as he starts shoving our stuff into the overnight bag.

Throwing my clothes onto the bed, he gets dressed, and my insides deflate. Looks like we're going home early.

Oh please, you knew the second you heard his father's voice.

Pulling my underwear on with a little pout, I try to think of something to ease this tension, but I've got nothing. Zander's pale expression and wrinkled forehead are killing me. I want to wipe away that frown... but I can't. Zander's football dreams are not turning out the way he planned, and he's so obviously gutted... and no doubt dreading the upcoming conversation with his father.

I want to save him from it. But I can't.

So I quietly brush my teeth, comb my hair, and walk out to find Zander stripping the bed.

"Any instructions on how to leave the place?"

"Uh... yeah." I blink, checking my phone and helping him leave the little cabin as instructed. I feel like crying as we lock the door and store the key again.

This is not how I wanted our overnighter to end.

I had hiking plans this morning. I'd bought special picnic treats. We were going to take the trail into the forest and perch on a rock, eating Pringles and staring out at the wintery landscape.

We weren't supposed to leave here until two.

Glancing over my shoulder, I give the cabin a morose smile and wave goodbye before hopping into the passenger seat.

Zander's already behind the wheel, looking anxious, checking his watch and tapping the steering wheel with his thumb.

As soon as I'm buckled up, he pulls away from the house, and I sit there quietly, listening to him tell me that everything's going to be okay.

"Dad was only yelling because of this football thing. He gets really paranoid and anxious over this kind of stuff. He's overreacting, as usual." Zander rolls his eyes. "As soon as we get that all figured out, he won't even care about our night away." His smile is reassuring, which is why I can't understand this unsettling maelstrom in my stomach. "I don't know what the hell's going on with Brighton, but I'm not going to be riding any benches. Dad and I will set up a meeting with the Brighton coach. It's all gonna be okay. I can play better than some other quarterback." He sounds like he's trying to convince himself right now. "And I'll impress everyone, and hell..." An awkward laugh punches out of him. "Maybe I can even go pro. How cool would that be?"

A smile spreads across his face, like he's genuinely pumped by that idea, and I'm sitting here wondering what happened to all the talk of traveling the world together.

Was that all bullshit?

I want to call him on it, but he's talking so fast, I can't find a break in conversation.

"Brighton wants me, Sparky. This is all just a big misunderstanding." He reaches for my hand, kissing my knuckles. "And then I'll only be a half-hour drive away. I can see you on the weekends."

When you don't have games or practices.

"And maybe you can come out one night a week for dinner or something."

When you're not studying or going to college events that I'm not invited to.

I worry my lip, trying to keep all my concerns in check.

"It's okay." He raises his hand, kissing my knuckles. "I know my dad can be scary sometimes, but I'm not going to let him yell at you or make you feel bad, okay? You didn't do anything wrong. Yesterday was seriously the best birthday I've ever had, and I'm gonna tell my father that."

Forcing a smile, I bob my head and try not to think too far ahead.

All I can focus on is surviving the day and making sure my happy face is in full play, because Zander's got enough on his plate without me being all emotional and needy.

CHAPTER 24
ZANDER

Sienna was pretty quiet on the way home. I was trying to keep my tone bright and positive, but it wasn't working. She was worried. Maybe even scared. I got it. My dad could be an ass. Which is why I'm going to drop her home first. Sure, I'd love her there when I deal with this bullshit about some other quarterback. I can't believe that! There's got to be a mix-up. The Coach from Brighton was keen on me. He said so himself.

Maybe this Coach Jones from Kelsey U is just lying because *he* wants me on his team. Whatever. I'm not moving that far away from my girlfriend. Brighton is the college for me, and I'm not going to let someone else take my spot.

Glancing at my girlfriend, I want to reassure her again that I won't be leaving her, but for some reason, the words won't come. Maybe she's more worried about my dad's reaction to her birthday surprise.

"I'm gonna drop you home first, okay?"

"You sure?" Her big blue eyes look kinda glassy. Shit, is she fighting tears?

I reach for her hand again. "It's okay, Sparks. You don't have to deal with my dad. I don't want him guilt-tripping you when you didn't do anything wrong."

Okay, so she lied for us.

But that's not a felony.

And she shouldn't be made to feel bad for doing something nice for me. It was my freaking birthday!

I hope I can talk my father around, but Sienna doesn't have to be a witness to that fight. I get the impression her family never raises their voices at each other, so it's best if I drop her home and deal with the shitstorm on my own.

She doesn't say anything as I pull up to her house. Flashing me a nervous smile, her lips wobble when she whispers, "Good luck."

"I'll walk you in." Jumping out of the car before she can stop me, I grab her backpack, carrying it to the front door.

It swings open before we reach it, and I can tell the second I spot Mr. Erling's face that he knows what we did.

"Shit," I mutter under my breath, bracing myself for the lecture.

"You are never to see my daughter again!"

"How dare you do that with her!"

"How dare you—"

"Hey, Dad." Sienna rises to her tiptoes, pecking his cheek before brushing past him.

He gives her a closed-mouth smile, then turns to me with a look that's... well, I don't know what it's telling me. Is he about to start yelling?

My shoulders tense, but all he does is let out a sigh and tip his head. "Come on in, kid. We need to talk."

"Double shit," I murmur under my breath as I follow him inside and find Sienna in the kitchen with her mother.

The woman has a stern look on her face, but it's hardly intimidating. Her eyes are too kind and playful—just like Sienna's. These people probably have no idea how to get truly pissed off about anything.

"So…" Mr. Erling clears his throat, taking a seat at the table and threading his fingers together. "Sounds like you two had an interesting evening."

Sienna winces. "What did you hear?"

"Well, I got myself a very irate phone call from Mr. Donohue this morning, telling me my daughter was leading her son astray and it's probably best that I keep you away from him."

"What?" I bristle, shoving my fists into my jacket pockets and storming toward the table. "That's bullshit! He can't make her do anything! And she's not leading me astray!"

Mrs. Erling raises her hands to calm me. "Sweetie, you don't need to yell any of that. We know." She nods, her smile soft as she points to the chair next to Sienna. "Sit down, Zander. It's okay. Let me make you two some cocoa."

"I don't think he has time for that, Mom," Sienna calls after her, rubbing her forehead and wincing again.

Turning back around, the woman glides back to the table and takes a seat. Looking at her daughter with a sad frown, she gently asks, "Did you really lie to us?"

Biting her lips together, Sienna blinks like she's fighting tears, then answers in a tiny voice. "Yes."

"Why?" Her dad sounds so hurt.

I watch his face bunch with disappointment and feel like shit.

Looking to my girlfriend, we share a pained smile before she admits, "I wasn't sure how you'd feel about me spending the night with my boyfriend." She shrugs. "But I just wanted to do something special for him. He's under so much pressure, and I thought he deserved a night away. And..." She looks at the table, picking at a dent in the wood. "I didn't want to share him with anyone else."

Her mother lets out a soft snicker. "Only-child syndrome. You've always been terrible at sharing your special treasures."

"He's the most special," she whispers, glancing at me with a soft blush.

Mr. Erling clears his throat. "How long have you two been sleeping together?"

I balk, my blood running cold as I throw him a jittery glance, then dart an SOS to Sienna.

She bites her lip, her nose wrinkling before she finally says, "About a month or so."

"Right." Mrs. Erling nods, eyeing me up and asking, "Are you being safe?"

"Yes, ma'am," I answer swiftly, my heart pulsing so hard, I can feel it between my ears.

Sienna nods, flashing me a nervous smile. "We use protection."

"Well... at least that's something." She tips her head and looks between us. "And you love each other?"

"Very much," we say in unison, then glance at each other and grin. It's so fucking obvious how we feel about each other, and I'm really hoping that's gonna score us some points here.

I'm still reeling that her dad isn't losing his shit and fisting my shirt, dragging me out of the house, and throwing me onto the lawn, screaming at me to never come near his precious girl again.

"I still think you're a little on the young side." Mr. Erling sighs. "Sex adds a whole new level to a relationship. It ups the emotion in a big way, and if things fall apart, it's gonna hurt so much worse."

"They're not going to fall apart," Sienna assures them. "We *love* each other. We're in this for the long haul."

"Sweetie." Mrs. Erling laughs. "You're only seventeen. How do you know this will last?"

"He's meant to be mine." Her blue gaze hits me then, confident with affection. "I can feel it in my bones, Mom. Zander and I are endgame."

A flash of skepticism crosses Mrs. Erling's face before she looks at me. "You think so?"

"Yes, ma'am." I nod, then turn to grin at my girlfriend. "Endgame." My throat suddenly feels thick, this hot buzz racing down my spine that I don't understand.

Of course we're endgame.

She's everything.

But you guys are so young.

Why our parents' logic is suddenly starting to hit me, I have no idea. Shaking my head, I rub my sweaty hands on my jeans and rise from the table. "Well, I better get home. The longer I leave it, the worse my old man's gonna get."

"Do you need me to come?" Sienna rises as well. Her skin is so pale, her eyes wide with fear.

"No, it's okay." I shake my head. "It's probably safer if I face the firing squad alone."

"Okay." She bites her bottom lip. "Well, can you maybe apologize on my behalf to them for... I don't know... doing something they didn't like?"

Resting my hand on her cheek, I block out the fact that her parents are watching us and quickly assure her, "*I* loved it, and I'm not apologizing for enjoying the best night of my life." I wink at her, loving the blush forming on her cheeks.

Her dad steps into my line of sight, catching my eye and throwing me a warning glare that makes me swallow.

"Sorry, sir," I mutter. "I promise I've always respected her, and—"

"He does." Sienna nods. "We're all about consent with each other, and—"

"And I don't need to hear any more." He raises his hands. "I don't want details."

"Good, because we don't want to give them to you." Sienna's face is all bunched up, and I can't help a soft snicker.

This is so fucking awkward. My skin's on fire, my heart is pounding, and I seriously need to get out of here.

Yet I love this family so much.

They're so calm and open and... they don't seem to hate me, even after they've found out I'm sleeping with their precious daughter.

204

"Before you go, just do me a favor, all right?" I stay by the table while Mrs. Erling crosses her arms and looks between me and Sienna. "Don't lie to us again. If you want to go away for a romantic night together... okay, so I probably would have said no, but the point is... don't lie to me. I hate it. I want to be able to trust you both, so please, next time... just tell us what you're up to, okay?"

My smile looks no doubt pained as I nod and then softly mutter, "I doubt there's going to be a next time if my parents have anything to say about it."

"Well, you're nearly a big college boy, so their say is going to lose some power soon enough." She winks at me, and I can't help grinning back.

"Thank you." I nod, then turn to Sienna. "Wish me luck."

"Luck." Her smile is sweet as she snuggles against my side. I wrap my arm around her and kiss the top of her head.

"I'll call you after, okay?"

"Okay." Her voice is soft, her blue eyes kind of sad when I go to pull away.

Taking her face, I cup those pretty cheeks and assure her once more. "Everything's going to be good. We'll make this work, okay?"

"Yeah." Her lips pull into a smile, and I kiss her, right there in front of her parents.

They don't seem to mind. I check their faces just before walking out the door and wish I could have grown up in a house like this one.

No yelling.

No pressure.

Just quiet conversation and bucketloads of acceptance.

If only.

CHAPTER 25
ZANDER

I've been inside Mom's house for all of one second when Dad starts yelling at me.

"What the hell were you thinking? Going off for a night with your girlfriend like you're on your fucking honeymoon? What is wrong with you? You're only eighteen! For fuck's sake, Zander!"

"Brett, stop yelling." Mom rolls her eyes, coming up behind him and glaring at me.

"I'm allowed to yell about this, Elise. If there is one time I can bawl my kid out, it's now. Come on! Twenty minutes ago, we were in full agreement."

"We are in agreement!" she bites back. "I just don't think yelling about it is going to help!"

"Fine, you want to deal with him? Go ahead! But look where your helicopter parenting has gotten us so far. You can't coddle him!"

"I'm not coddling anybody! I'm just trying to talk like a mature adult! Something you're failing to do with all your shouting!" She screams the words, and now I'm rolling my eyes as I brush past their argument and head up to my room.

They thunder up behind me, and I feel my shoulders bristle when I walk into my room and spot my open laptop on the desk with my email up on the screen.

"Were you checking my email?" I spin to glare at Dad.

"I was just seeing if you'd heard back from any other colleges. We're in crisis mode here, Zander! Brighton is a no-go, and we need to look at your options."

"This is my room. My space. *My* computer. And what the hell do you mean, Brighton is a no-go? They want me."

"And they want some other guy too! A quarterback they say has been performing better this season. A quarterback they're going to give all their time and attention to. Your ass will be sitting on that bench. No game time. No opportunities to show future scouts how good you are. All you'll be able to do is sit there praying the other guy gets injured!"

"Brett, that's awful." Mom glares at him, then shoots me a sympathetic smile. "I'm sorry, baby."

I squeeze my eyes shut, pinching the bridge of my nose while my insides flail. "How do you know all this stuff?"

Dad huffs. "Coach Jones called me this morning. He got wind of Brighton's interest in the guy they've been scouting. He's had a stronger season than you. Plus, he's got great charisma. The crowd seems to love him, and he interviews well. He's the kind of player who makes a school look really good."

And now my insides are deflating.

"Brighton thinks he'll be a better fit for them, and a sponsor has come out of the woodwork ready to back this kid all the way."

I open my mouth to response to that, but... I've got nothing.

Sponsors? No sponsors have ever approached me.

Shit, this is like a thunder punch to my ego.

"Now, Coach Jones is a good man. He seems really genuine, and he's keen to talk to you. He says you've got great potential, he likes your attitude better, and with a little training and a lot more focus, you can be the more dynamic player. He's assured me that you won't be riding the bench the whole season. He wants you out on the field. I doubt Brighton will say the same."

"But Brighton," I mumble, my grand plans disintegrating before me. "I want Brighton."

Dad scoffs and shakes his head. "Don't be an idiot. Brighton's not going to give you any game time! Kelsey U wants you, Zander. They'll train you and turn you into a better player!"

"But it's miles away."

"Oh for fuck sake!" Dad throws his arms up. "That girl has put some kind of spell on you! You're seriously standing there telling me you'd rather freeze your ass off on the sidelines and waste your entire college football career because of a five-hour drive? You're not thinking straight!" He taps his forehead with an agitated finger. "Shit, Zander! She's screwing up your life!"

His voice starts to rumble like a thunderstorm, and I raise my hand to shut him up. "I get it, Dad. You're pissed, but she's not screwing up anything."

His glare could melt tungsten, and I look away from it, crossing my arms to shield myself against the next attack.

"You were supposed to be at Noah's house," he hisses. "She stole you away, lied to everyone about it... and you just let her!"

"Dad—"

"You have no idea how disappointing it is to think your son is somewhere and then find out he lied to you and took off for a night away like he's a fully grown adult."

"I *am* a fully grown ad—"

"No, you're not!" he barks. "And don't even try to deny it. You think you're so grown up, but Zander... you're not. You don't pay your own bills, you don't buy your own groceries. You're not even old enough to drink yet! Practically everything you own was paid for by your mother or me! If you're so grown-up, you wouldn't have tricked everybody and gone behind our backs. That little girlfriend of yours is quite the schemer."

"Don't talk about her like that," I warn him.

Mom scoffs. "How can we not? This was all her idea!"

"Yeah, and it was a good one," I argue back, but my voice is a quiet mumble.

Mom closes her eyes with a huff. "Zander, you are too young to be spending a night away with a girl. For God's sake, you only turned eighteen yesterday! You might technically be an adult now, but you're certainly not acting like one! You're still in high school, and you shouldn't be sleeping together! You're too young! You're just too young!" Her voice starts to pitch, and I know exactly why she's getting so worked up.

With a soft sigh, I assure her, "We're being safe. We're using protection. You don't need to get so stressed about this. I'm not going to get her pregnant. I love her, okay? I love her."

"It's not always about love," Dad mutters. "Love is just an emotion. You need to start using your head." He taps his hair with his finger, then thrusts his phone at me. "Now let's call Coach Jones back and get this shit sorted."

"I'd rather talk to Coach Watkins from Brighton." I cross my arms and glare back at him.

"Fine." Dad huffs. "Let's call him and find out what the hell is going on. Maybe hearing the truth from him will help you get your head on straight."

My parents gather in front of me, and the weight of their gazes suddenly feels too much to bear. I stare at the phone in Dad's hand and finally take it. Part of me wants to ask him to make the call, but I can't go claiming I'm an adult and then expect him to fix my problems for me.

Shit.

With shaking fingers, I find Coach Watkins's number and hit Call. He answers after five long rings.

"Mr. Donohue. What can I do for you?"

"Put it on speaker," Dad whisper-barks, and I give him a sharp side-eye before giving in to his request.

"Hey, Coach Watkins. It's me, Zander. Sorry to call you on the weekend."

"Not a problem. I understand this is an anxious time for players like yourself. If you're wondering about your letter of intent, you are on our list. I'm keen to come and meet with your family to discuss details, and I was going to book a time next week."

"Thank you for that, sir." I give my dad a pointed look.

He rolls his eyes and snatches the phone out of my hand. "Coach, it's Brett here. Before Zander signs anything, I want to clear something up with you…"

There's a pregnant pause, which I was kinda hoping Coach Watkins would fill. His ominous silence is doing nothing to ease my tattered nerves.

Dad clears his throat. "I've heard a rumor that Zander isn't the only quarterback you're speaking to. We're concerned he's going to be riding the bench all year."

"I see." That's all Coach says, and his following silence is even louder than the first one.

My shoulders slump, and I share a pained frown with my father.

"Coach Watkins, we really need some clarification on this." Dad's tone is so strong and assertive… and for once, I'm actually grateful for it.

"Look, I don't know what to tell you here, Brett. We're keen to have Zander on the team, but yes, he's not the only quarterback we're hoping to sign. It's good to have backup players. Zander will still be getting all the same training and quality coaching."

"But no game time."

"I thought you wanted me?" I can't help butting in. "You said last year that—"

"Yeah, and last year you were playing like a pro. This season hasn't been as strong, and it's forced us to check out other players. I don't know what to tell you, kid. You're slipping, and I do believe you have the potential to get back to where you were, but I can't risk only signing you."

The air in my lungs goes cold, my mind blanking out as Dad takes over the rest of the call and I stand there listening to his disappointment, his arguments, and then telling Coach Watkins he can shove it and to not bother setting up a meeting because I won't be signing with a school that doesn't appreciate me.

Mom gasps and I blink, snapping out of my stupor in time to see Dad hanging up.

"What did you...?" My words trail off as I gape at my father's thundering anger.

"If they're not going to give you any game time, they can't have you!" he growls.

"But Dad, I... I can prove myself during practices. I can..." I wince, running a hand through my hair. "This can't be right."

"Why not, Zander?" Dad's tone is cutting, and I wish I hadn't looked up to face him just before he said it. His eyes are burning two holes right through my skull, and I feel ripped apart, exposed. "Why can't it be right when you've been slacking off? You just had your worst season ever!"

"But... they liked me. He said I was good."

"Last season! *Last* season you were good enough. But not anymore. Someone else has come through the woodwork and shone brighter than you." His scathing voice slaps me hard, and I lean away from him, still struggling to believe this.

I had it all mapped out, and now... I'm not going to Brighton.

What the fuck am I supposed to do now?

Dad sighs. "We need to call Coach Jones back and at

least secure a place at Kelsey U. We haven't heard back from the other colleges we sent your tapes to, so you're down to one option." Shaking his head, Dad gives me a disappointed frown. "I wanted you to have choices, son. And now you're all out of them."

"I don't want to go to Kelsey U. I don't—"

"You're going to Kelsey U." Dad glares down at me. "You are meeting with Coach Jones, and you are going to assure him that you will work harder for him than you've ever worked for anybody. And when they send you a letter of intent, you're signing it."

"But they're miles away!"

"I don't give a shit. You're going, Zander. I won't let you throw your life away over a girl. The school you wanted didn't work out. You need to get over yourself and start thinking about your future, because I am warning you now... if you think that being with your girlfriend is going to solve all your problems, you're wrong. A relationship is only one small aspect of your life, and you can't design your entire world around it, because it will fall apart on you, and then what are you left with?"

I swallow, not wanting to answer that question, but my mother goes ahead.

"A painful divorce and a whole lot of heartache. Don't put yourself through it." Her voice is bitter as she storms out of the room, slamming the door shut behind her.

Dad flinches but stands tall, glaring out the window. I watch his nostrils flare, that muscle in his jaw ticking, before staring morosely at the floor.

Coach Watkins doesn't want me after all.

Well, he's still willing to take you... if you want to ride the bench. But that's not good enough for Dad, and... shit, maybe it's not good enough for me either.

"You love football. I know you do."

I swallow, unwilling to respond to my father's quiet statement.

"And I know you love this girl, too, but she'll still be here when you get back... and football won't. This is your shot, Zander. Please, don't fuck it up."

Shoving my hands into my pockets, I clench my teeth and force myself to breathe.

"I'll call Coach Jones back soon. I just need a drink first," Dad mutters.

"I don't want that school," I stubbornly mumble. "I'm not moving there."

"Zander, you don't have a choice!" he snaps. "I get that this Sienna girl is everything to you right now and you can't stand the thought of living apart from her. But you can't throw your life away for some romantic notion. If you're really meant to be together, then you can handle the distance."

I grit my teeth, hating every one of his words.

After a thick beat, Dad lets out a heavy sigh.

For the first time since I walked in the door, his tone drops to one of sympathy. "I get that you're disappointed, and I'm sorry it's not working out the way you wanted. But please, son... I'm begging you... go and explore the world. Find out who you are. Experience life as an independent man." I glance up in time to see his eyes glass with pain. "Don't make the same mistakes I did."

My forehead bunches into a sharp frown.

"Don't get me wrong." He reaches out to pat my arm.

"I love Monica. She's my daughter—of course I love her. But my life would have turned out very differently if she hadn't come along when she did. I probably would have broken up with your mother before graduating from college, and we both would have discovered ourselves and figured out that we weren't the right fit."

"Sienna *is* the right fit," I grit out.

"How do you know that when you haven't experienced anything else? She's your first, right?"

I swallow, then nod.

"And she might be your last," he tries to appease me. "But... I just want you to be sure. I want you to get out of this town and have some adventures. I want you to discover all this world has to offer and truly know what you want before you get locked in the way I did."

I scoff and shake my head.

"I'm just trying to save you from a lot of pain and heartache. That's all I'm doing."

"You think leaving her won't be painful?" I glare at him.

Dad's expression buckles, his eyes glassing over again. "Try having two kids with her first. Try molding your whole life around her only to discover that you're making each other miserable. Try looking back on your life and realizing how many opportunities you let pass you by. You live with that regret for a while... and then we can talk about pain, okay?"

He slaps my shoulder, then stalks out of my room.

I glare at his back until my door clicks shut behind him and all that I'm left with is a thrumming silence that wants to bury me.

CHAPTER 26
SIENNA

It's been a rough few months. Zander's parents have really restricted his movements, and I'm hardly getting to see him at all. His father has him training any chance he can get... and Zander's letting him boss him around. I hate it, but the few times I've said something, my boyfriend has cut the conversation short and changed the subject.

The fact that he didn't get into Brighton was a kick in the balls. He ended up signing with Kelsey U, and although he forced a smile for the cameras on signing day, I could tell he wasn't super excited. I guess he's relieved somewhere was willing to take him, but shouldn't he be totally pumped?

The coaches at Kelsey U have given him the hard word, set the expectations so freaking high. They see his potential, but only if he's willing to give them his all. They want to mold him into a pro athlete... and he's going to let them.

But is that what he really wants?

I honestly can't tell.

Kelsey U is so freaking far away. It's still within the state of Idaho, but it's not like we'll get to see each other very often.

Zander had no choice but to accept. After he called to tell me, I couldn't help crying myself to sleep.

I'm gutted but trying not to let it show. I know the reality of long distance. Last night, when we were talking on the phone, I was trying to be happy for him, and I went on about how easy it will be. We can stay in touch on the daily. It'll be totally fine.

But is that honestly true?

He's going to get caught up in college life. And I want that for him. I want him to enjoy his time.

"It's only a year, baby," Mom tried to comfort me. "You can apply to the same place, and then you'll be together. In fact, it's not even a year if you take into account all the school breaks. It's hardly any time at all."

That did actually make me feel better... and maybe we can do this.

If we can survive his parents' restrictions, surely we can survive a year apart. Thanks to a tightened curfew, I'm only getting to see my man for one night on the weekends and the odd lunch hour when he's not studying in the library or working out.

His parents are still annoyed that we're sleeping together and have tried everything in their power to make sure we're never alone or without adult supervision. Thankfully, my parents are a little more relaxed, although it's not like they're encouraging us to get a room. I still have to leave my door open when we're at my place.

They're not mad about the fact that we've had sex, but my parents definitely think we're too young, so they're not exactly accommodating a repeat, you know?

Which is why we're parked up at Harrison Point. It's become one of our favorite spots, because hardly anyone ever comes here. It's about the only place on Earth we can get some privacy these days, and this is usually where we end our date nights.

We only have one hour left until Zander's due home, and we're making out like crazy, his hands roaming my body as we make the most of our time together.

He leaves for football camp tomorrow.

Zander's driving away from me tomorrow morning, doing the five-hour trip with his dad to go and train with the college football team.

He really needs to shine at this camp or he's going to get zero game time. Coach Jones has assured him he'll get to play a few games... if he performs well during practices, so the pressure is on. If he can show them what he's got this week, then he's got a chance to turn everything around for himself.

I really want that for him. I know how much he loves football, and I want him to be happy.

But I hate the thought of him leaving.

He doesn't really want to go. The camp sounds super strict. They're not allowed their phones or anything. It's an intense week of training and bonding... and there's no room for me.

Dammit. I was so pumped for spring break and all the things we were going to do together, but my best-laid plans were washed away in a heartbeat. Now I've only got the next hour before he's gone. And I don't know if I want to spend it making love or snuggling or playing silly games or…

His tongue glides against mine and I whimper, holding on to him for dear life.

It's only a week, Sienna. Stop being so dramatic.

I wish I could explain why I'm feeling so unsettled by all of this. It's only a week. Logically, I really am making a big deal out of nothing, but I can't seem to stop myself. My stomach has been in knots for weeks, like I'm waiting for some kind of impending doom. Maybe it's just the fact that I know Zander's parents are against our relationship.

Whatever it is, I don't want to say goodbye to my boyfriend tonight.

"You're so sexy, baby," Zander moans between kisses.

I'm straddling his lap in the back seat of his car. My shirt's open, my bra pulled down so he can do what he likes with my eager nipples. I love how his thumbs brush over them as he nuzzles my neck. I grind against his erection, knowing this is happening and needing that connection more than anything.

"I want you inside me," I whisper, lightly biting his earlobe.

He hums in his throat, bucking his hips with a soft laugh before I scramble off his knee and unzip him. His dick springs out to greet me and I grin, kneeling on the seat beside him so I can suck his head.

Lightly fisting the back of my hair, he groans and rocks into me before reaching down my body and pushing my panties aside. His finger nudges into my entrance and I lose concentration, moaning against his cock while he finds my sweet spot and teases the life out of it.

Licking his erection, I grip his leg and pant, whimpering as that sensation I love so much starts working its way through my entire body, spreading that blinding heat down to my toes and up to my head until I'm—

"Oh my... oh my—ohhhh..." My body starts to convulse as he buries his fingers between my legs, then guides my head up so I can kiss him.

His tongue is perfect, my humming body wet and ready for him.

"Gotta have you now, baby," he mumbles against my lips, lifting me onto his lap and lining us up.

I sink onto him, and we let out a luxurious moan. Yeah, I really do adore this.

Staring into his eyes, I smile at him, bouncing on him a few times while he tucks my hair behind my ear, then glides his hands up my thighs. Biting his lip, he looks like a sexy model, tipping his head back and enjoying the ride. I lick his throat, gliding my tongue over his Adam's apple before finding his mouth again.

He feels so good.

I love the way he fills me.

I love the heat and the slick and the—

"Condom," I gasp, pulling away from him. "We need to wrap you, buddy."

"Shit." He winces. "Sorry. I forgot."

"That's okay. I did too." Reluctantly rising off him, I wait impatiently on my knees, my body tingling with urgency as he pulls out a condom and wraps himself. My body is bobbing by the time he's finally done, and when he turns to resume what we started, I decide to be a little adventurous and spin around. Glancing out the window, I check that we're on our own and turn back with a mischievous wink.

"What are you up to, Sparky?"

"Come on." I giggle, jumping out of the car and beckoning him to follow me.

He checks the area, stepping out and making sure we're hidden in the shadows before turning to face me. I'm propped against the car, my pale ass glowing in the moonlight as I offer myself to him in a way I never have before.

He shuffles up behind me, his jeans still bunched around his ankles. Resting his hands on my ass, he checks, "Are you sure?"

"Yeah." I grin over my shoulder. "We've never done this before, and I want to try it."

"Okay," he murmurs, and my insides buzz with anticipation as he glances around again to make sure we're alone before lining up his dick.

I have to help him. This new angle is a little different, and—

"Oh fuck," I gasp, my insides blooming with pleasure as he spears me from behind. "Oh wow, that feels amazing." I can barely get the words out as I rest my head against the cold metal of his trunk and fight a giddy laugh. Why haven't we tried this before?

Zander groans, holding my hips and pumping a little faster.

The cool night air kisses our exposed skin, and I can feel a fresh orgasm building as our slick coupling takes us both over the edge. It's fast and intense, this new sensation ripping through me as I join myself to this guy I love so freaking much.

He comes faster than usual, his thrusts turning chaotic and frenzied as he quickly reaches climax and buries himself until I can feel him all the way to my core.

Talk about being one.

I seriously can't get enough of this.

Standing back up, I lean against him, turning my head to kiss him while he's still inside me.

"That was fucking amazing," he pants, kissing me and marveling the same way I am. "We definitely have to do that again."

"Oh yeah." I let out a soft laugh before flopping back against his car, loving the way his big hands caress my naked ass and lower back.

I want to ask him if we can just stay out here all night, making love and being together.

But I know that's an impossible dream.

Our time is running out. Very soon I'll be kissing him goodbye, and then he'll be driving out of my life for a whole week!

CHAPTER 27
ZANDER

So, I didn't know how to feel about football camp. It was with a college I didn't even want to attend, so that put me in a bit of a foul mood over it all. Plus, there was the whole driving there with my dad bit. He wouldn't let me go alone… probably because he was worried I'd bail and sneak away with Sienna for the week.

Okay, so the thought had crossed my mind, but I never would have actually gone through with it.

As much as I hate my dad's constant diatribes and worries about my future, I do secretly agree with him that I need a college education.

I think the whole breaking up with Sienna thing is bullshit, and as hard as my parents have tried, they are still losing that battle. I love my girlfriend, and I'm not dumping her because of their insane fears.

We can do long distance for a year. It's not that big a deal.

I'll go to this college and play some ball. I'll do what I

have to, graduate like they keep going on about, and then Sienna and I can do whatever the fuck we want.

Unless you go pro. Coach Jones thinks you've got what it takes.

This new college doesn't have the same caliber of football as Brighton does, but it's still a good school, and Coach Jones has a good rep, apparently.

Shit, maybe I do need to throw my all into this thing. The fact that I wasn't accepted anywhere but here has kind of knocked me. Maybe I did fuck around too much in my last year. Maybe I did let Sienna distract me. But like hell I'm blaming her.

I love her.

She's my girl.

Nothing my parents say is going to change that.

We arrive at Kelsey U and I reluctantly get out of Dad's car, hitching my pants and hating the flood of nerves trying to drown me.

"You can do this, son. You're gonna be great." Dad gives me a stiff nod but softens it with a smile. He's proud of me for doing this, and it's nice to be in his good books for once. I follow him into the stadium.

The sun is shining and the field is looking perfect, the green grass vibrant as guys in training gear run around completing drills. I watch the quarterback hurl his pass down the field. It's a pretty good spiral, but I know I can throw better than that... and it's time for me to prove it.

Fired up in a way I haven't been in a while, I shake Coach Jones's hand and am pulled into a world of football... that I have the best time in.

I'm introduced to the entire coaching team. The head

coach—Miles Filmore—seems pretty awesome, and the players all respect him as far as I can tell. Coach Jones works the offensive players hard, and there are mumbled complaints, but I can tell he only wants the best out of his players.

Dad isn't allowed to stay and watch, thank fuck, and not having him in the stands analyzing my every mood is liberating. No one knows me here. There are no expectations. I can write myself anew, and it feels fucking fantastic.

The guys on my new team are friendly and fun. The seniors welcome me into the fold. They're obviously really good at looking out for the newbies. I spend the first day hanging out with the starting quarterback and wide receiver. I've never felt so welcomed and appreciated before.

I'm housed in a dorm with a bunch of football guys and am bunking with a freshman who tells me story after story about his epic year so far. I can't lap it up fast enough. He takes me to a mixer, shows me all the best food spots around campus, and opens my eyes to a whole new world.

It's fucking amazing.

I've never known anything like it. This place is so huge. There's so much to do, see, experience. And it's great not having a parent breathing down my neck.

If I'm really honest with myself, it's also kind of nice not having any pressure from Sienna either. She doesn't mean to do it, but when I spot her big sad eyes watching me walk past at school and I can't stop to kiss her or say hi, it always makes me feel bad. Or when I'm not allowed to go see her and she sends me crying-face emojis... I know she's only kidding, but it still feels like I'm letting her down.

She texts me all the time, and I love it. I do. But it can be a lot, too, you know?

I thought I'd hate the phone ban this week. I said it was the stupidest rule. They want full immersion to build team camaraderie, and I mocked them for it. But... it's been awesome.

No one can reach me here.

It's just me, football, and a bunch of awesome guys I'm determined to impress.

CHAPTER 28
SIENNA

Things have been different since Zander got back from camp. He's been slightly distant, and I can see his eyes light up whenever he gets a text or Snap for any of the college guys he met during training. He had the best time and came home elated... like seriously. Basically, all our conversations for our first few dates after he got back were all about that week. At least the stuff he could tell me. Apparently, there are a bunch of "boys only" secrets that he isn't allowed to share.

It felt so freaking grade school, but I didn't want to hassle him about it. The way he talks about that week is so animated and enthusiastic, like this camp has brought him back to life again. He's pumped and so excited for the new school year to begin. Now, he can't wait to graduate and get prepped for this next big adventure.

I'm trying to be the supportive girlfriend here, but it's getting harder and harder.

He had so much fun without me, and I was fucking miserable.

I spent the first two days after he left crying because I wouldn't be able to text or interact with him for an entire week. I wrote him letters instead, pouring out everything I was feeling, painting out our dreams of world travel and a life together.

But when he got back all pumped and excited, I couldn't find the courage to give them to him. It suddenly dawned on me that the last thing he'd want is pages of sappy love letters.

Ugh, it made me feel so needy and pathetic.

How have I become this girl?

"And how the hell am I meant to cope if he's away for an entire year?" I whine to Olivia, who is so over me she's not even bothering to hide her eye rolls anymore. "He's going to move on, Liv. He's going to forget about me, and I'll be left behind."

"Yeah, that really sucks." She doesn't sound like she means it, and I turn on her with a frown.

"Just say whatever it is you're trying not to say!" I snap.

"Okay, fine!" She slaps her magazine closed and growls at me. "You're being pathetic. I get that you're in love, I do. But you're seventeen. You have your whole life ahead of you, and you should be focusing on all the cool stuff you're going to get to do next year. We're going to be seniors! And yes, you'll be missing Zander, but if you're going to be this mopey, weepy girl who doesn't want to get excited about any of the cool things we'll be doing, I'm not sure I want to hang out with you anymore!"

I gasp, horrified that she just came out and said that to me.

You just told her to! You practically dared her to be blatantly honest with you!

I blink, fighting off a round of scorching tears and glaring at the wall while I try not to yell at her for being a lousy friend.

"He can't be your whole world, Sienna."

"He is my world," I mumble. "He's everything."

"Then you've made your world too small," she mutters. "And might I remind you that you have a bunch of other really cool people in your life who are fun to be with too. You've made everything about him. It's too intense."

"But I love him." I turn to her, tears trickling out of my eyes. I don't bother brushing them away; more will soon follow.

"And that's great." Her expression softens. "But you can love other stuff too. There's room for more than just him. And you should know that better than anyone. You've been all over the world." She flings her arms wide, and I don't have it in me to try and explain it to her.

She doesn't get it because she's grown up in the same house on the same street going to school with the same people she grew up with. She doesn't know how hard it is to make connections when you're new. She doesn't know what it's like to be untethered all the time.

Zander's the first person—aside from my parents—who has ever made me feel truly grounded.

I love him.

He's my person.

My endgame.

I can feel him slipping away from me. And it's killing me.

Hugging my knees to my chest, I sniff and let the tears fall. Olivia sighs and continues flicking through her magazine, her movements sharp and snappy.

I endure it for as long as I can, until my nerves are strung out so tight that I want to scream at her to read her magazine more quietly.

Yep, I have to get out of here.

"I'm gonna go," I say, grabbing my bag and flinging it over my shoulder.

She doesn't fight me or beg me to stay. If anything, she looks bored as I mumble my goodbyes and run out of her house.

Ugh. The next school year is going to suck!

This town is too small and narrow.

I want to go with Zander. I want to follow him to a new adventure!

But I'm not invited. I still have to graduate from high school. And it's so obvious that he wants to go and pursue this football thing on his own. He hasn't outright said it, but I just get this sense that he's way more excited about this upcoming year than I am.

Kicking stones, I watch them scuttle down the street as I amble back home. I want to swing past Zander's place and see him, but he's in the throes of studying for all his finals right now, and I'm not allowed anywhere near him.

He'll get his phone back at the end of the day, and we can text for a while, but it won't be enough to heal this ache inside me.

I miss my boyfriend.
I'm dreading next year.
And no one seems to get it.

CHAPTER 29
ZANDER

I spend the afternoon studying. It sucks, and I'm so over the books by the time I'm finally allowed my phone back.

My first thought is to call Sienna. I miss her voice and that sweet laugh of hers. I want to make up stupid stories with her and watch her face on the screen.

But the second I turn it on, my screen lights up with a stream of notifications from the Kelsey U Titans. With a grin, I take a few minutes to react to them all, commenting back and sending stupid GIFs, then getting even funnier GIFs in reply.

It cracks me up, and I'm lying on my bed laughing when my phone starts to vibrate with a call from Sienna.

"Oh shit." I wince, feeling bad for forgetting about her. "Hey, Sparky," I answer with a grin, drinking in her pretty face.

Her blue eyes are so open and beautiful. And that smile. Shit, I can't get enough of that smile.

"Hey." Her dimple pops into place. "How was studying?"

"Yeah, good. My brain has officially melted, but I'm still breathing."

She giggles and I bunch the pillow under my chin, lying on my stomach and watching her as she eats a cookie, licking crumbs off her lips.

I wish I could lick those lips too.

"I miss you," I murmur. "I miss your lips."

Her smile is sunshine. "I miss your lips too. And your hands and your body and your voice and..." Her eyes suddenly glass over. "I miss all of you."

That pout of hers, normally so cute, is like a knife blade through the chest.

"Sen, don't cry. Please."

"I'm sorry," she snivels, slashing tears off her cheeks. "Everything's just so different now. You're so busy and I never get to see you, and you'll be going away soon and... it's gonna be hard."

"Yeah," I croak, knowing how right she is.

I'm gonna be caught up with football and college. Having to stay in touch with her—as much as I love it—is gonna be another pressure. I can't risk losing all the ground I made during that football camp. I've got to stay in good with my team and find a place in that college.

Will Sienna hold me back from doing that? Will my obligation to her be at war with what I want to achieve with this new team?

And how is that fair for her? Having a boyfriend she can't rely on? Feeling like she's being fit in rather than top priority?

My stomach twists into an uncomfortable knot as I try to comfort my girlfriend. "We just need to focus on one day at a time. We've got this festival coming up. That's gonna be awesome."

"Yeah." She sniffs. "Only one month to go."

"That's right, baby. Then it's you in a bikini and some little cut-off shorts and me rocking out to all my favorite bands."

"*Our* favorite bands." She giggles. "And what will you be wearing? Can I expect some kind of ripped-off shorts or bikini from you?"

I snort and shake my head. "No point me wearing anything fancy. They'll all be too busy checking out my hot girlfriend."

She blushes. "But you're not gonna let any of them touch me, right?"

"That's right, baby. You are all mine."

"Yes, I am." She kisses the screen, and I grin back at her smile.

Shit, she is so fucking beautiful.

And she is mine.

That feeling should make me want to fly. I've got the prettiest girl in the world for a girlfriend!

So why does my heart hurt right now?

What's with the boulder in my chest?

"WE BROKE UP"

CHAPTER 30
SIENNA

I already know what he's going to say before he even says it. I can tell by the look on his face, that sadness in his eyes. He can't quite look at me properly, and I know... deep down in my gut... I know.

I guess I've known for weeks, but I've just been playing pretend. Enjoying the summer and acting like there's nothing looming ahead of us.

But the time has come.

Zander leaves for college in six days, and I know what he's about to do.

Sitting on my bed, I grab a pillow from behind me and nestle it on my lap, playing with the corner of the pillowcase and gnawing on my bottom lip.

"Thing is..." He sighs, running a hand through my hair. "How do I do this?"

You don't.

You stay with me and say screw college!

You remember that perfect weekend we had at the music festival!

My mind jumps back to those three days of pure bliss. For some bizarre reason, his parents had finally been okay with us going. Maybe Zander argued for weeks to get their approval, I don't know, but we drove off to that big field in the middle of nowhere and rocked out to a bunch of bands. Thousands of people were there, but there was only me and Zander. We laughed, we sang, we made love in our little tent.

One of the afternoons, I covered my naked body with Nerds and laughed as he licked them off, teasing me for my bad taste in candy before plunging into me with powerful thrusts that left me breathless.

We slept naked and woke up against each other—hot and sweaty. We splashed around in the creek, me in my little bikini. We even snuck into the woods and I rode him while he sat against a tree trunk telling me I was the most beautiful girl he's ever known.

And now he's breaking up with me.

"It's not like I want to do this. I just think it's for the best, you know?" He stops pacing from my closet to my bed and crouches down, begging me with a look I can't stomach.

I grit my teeth, willing myself not to cry.

"I'm gonna be so busy at college, and I don't want you to feel let down by me. I don't want to hold you back either. You're about to start your senior year, and that's supposed to be fun and amazing. I don't want you pining for me and feeling sad all the time." He winces, his expression buckling as he softly murmurs, "But I don't want to let you go either."

"Then don't." I snatch his wrist when he stands up again. "Don't let me go."

"Sen," he rasps, his eyes glassing as he gazes down at me. His smile is heartbreaking, and I can't deny my tears anymore.

They bubble up inside me, and I close my eyes, letting the first few fall.

His thumb is light on my cheek as he brushes them away. "I love you," he whispers. "I'll always love you."

"Then why are you doing this?"

"Because I..." He huffs. "Fuck! I hate that I'm about to say this, but I think our parents are right. We *are* young, and we haven't experienced all life has to offer yet. If I don't break up with you, you're going to apply to Kelsey U whether you want to go there or not. I know that's what you're gonna do. Because you want to be close to me."

"What's so wrong with that?" I flick my hand up in the air. "I don't even know what I want to study, so what difference does it make where I go to college?"

"You can't make your whole life about me... just like I can't make mine about you." He plunks onto the edge of my bed, gathering up my hand and playing with my fingers. "We can't be each other's *everything*. We need to figure out what makes us happy outside of our relationship too. I can't be your only dream. That won't satisfy you long term. And I'm worried if we stay together that we'll end up bitter and annoyed. I never want to resent you."

It's a punch to the stomach, and I quickly draw my hand out of his grasp.

I miss his touch instantly, but I'm also fighting the urge to kick him off my bed.

We're not his parents! What the hell?

Here I am, brought to life by this guy, and he's feeling like we're weighing each other down. Holding each other back.

"I didn't realize we were such a burden to each other," I mutter.

"Sen, I didn't mean it that way."

"No, it's okay. I get it. You want to go off and be an adult. You don't want to be tied down by some immature high school girl, right?"

"Please, don't take it like that. I'm setting us both free."

I gape at him. It's impossible to hide my hurt, and I can see he instantly regrets the way he just worded that.

Tears scorch my eyes again, my heart pounding like a bass drum as I throw my pillow at him, jumping off the bed and yelling, "I don't feel caged! I'm not trapped in this thing the way you so obviously are!" Storming to my door, I fling it open and growl, "You want to be free? Then go! Leave! Do whatever the fuck you want!"

"Sienna." My words are hurting him, and I hate that broken look on his face right now, but can't he see how much this is killing me?

My stomach jerks and rumbles as I try to fight the sobs threatening to punch out of me. "I love you," I whimper, covering my mouth with my hand and muffling my words. "I'll only ever love you."

His expression folds as he stands up, rushing over to me and gathering me in his arms. "Then you don't have anything to worry about. Because if we're meant to be, we're gonna happen. I'm just asking for a time-out so I can focus on my first year at Kelsey U and you can focus on having the best senior year."

My fingers curl into his shirt, and I sniff against his shoulder.

"I need to make football my priority right now. We'll have a clean break to start, really give us a chance to get on with our lives, and then once the season's over...we can reassess. I'm not trying to break your heart, Sienna. I love you, okay?" Leaning back, he holds my face in his hands and silently begs me to believe him. "I love you. You're my girl."

"Not if you break up with me."

He swears under his breath, resting his forehead against mine. "I'm trying to do the right thing here. For both of us."

Letting go of his shirt, I sniff again, feeling this odd numbness travel over me. He's not going to change his mind. I can feel it. There's nothing I can say or do to make him bend.

This is over.

For a season or a year or forever, I don't know.

But for now... we're done.

I stand there in that knowledge for I don't know how long, fighting tears and whimpering quietly against the door. He holds my face, brushing his thumbs along my cheekbones and not saying a damn thing.

It takes everything in me to finally find the strength to push him away.

I gently nudge him back, crossing my arms and shrinking away from him. "You should go."

"Sen—"

"It's time for you to go." I nod, then sniff again. "Go."

"Please, I don't want to—"

"Go, Zander! Just go!"

He jerks away from my sudden scream, blinking at me like I've lost my mind before stumbling away from me.

I squeeze my arms until I can feel my nails digging into my skin, leaving sharp indents that hurt. But I can't let up.

After a beat of unbearable silence, Zander finally shows a little mercy and walks out of my room.

As soon as I hear the front door shut downstairs, I run to my bed, fling myself onto it, and let those gut-wrenching sobs break free.

CHAPTER 31
ZANDER

I've been feeling like shit ever since I ended things with Sienna. That look on her face when she asked me to go... fuck, I knew she probably flung herself onto her bed as soon as I left and cried her heart out.

I cried too.

She probably wouldn't believe me if I told her, but I did.

When I walked through my dad's front door, he took one look at my face and knew.

"You did it."

"Yeah." My voice broke, and he stood from the table, walking around to wrap his arms around me.

I wasn't used to hugs from my old man, but he squeezed the back of my neck and held me as I broke apart and cried like a fucking baby.

It's the weirdest thing, but since football camp, Dad and I have been getting along better. He was really proud of all that I achieved that week. Coach Jones must have talked me up big-time, because Dad's been all smiles and praise.

And now I've gone and done the last thing he wanted me to do, and I could feel his pride as he held me tight and let me mourn.

After that cryfest, I took the longest shower. I stayed in that steaming box until my skin was bright red and wrinkled. It didn't make me feel any better.

I couldn't sleep that night, and I haven't slept well any night since.

I miss my girl.

I hate that we're not together anymore.

The number of times I grab my phone to text or call her. Maybe tell her a joke or send her a funny reel I saw on Instagram.

But I can't go doing that now, can I?

I won't do that asshole thing where I tease her with kindness only to break her heart all over again. It's better to just leave her alone so we can both get over each other.

I'm just not sure if I'll ever get over her.

But this is my choice, and I have to bear the pain. I'm doing the right thing. I have to believe that.

I've spent my days packing up my stuff, living between the two houses so my parents both feel like they've gotten their turn with me. We even went out for a fancy dinner as a family. Monica showed up as a surprise, and we had the best meal we've had... maybe ever. There was no fighting or tension. There was laughter and shared memories. And when we turned to the ugly topics of breakups, things stayed surprisingly amicable. Even

Monica admitted that she felt Sienna and I were getting too intense.

"I met a guy in my third year at college who I was completely besotted with. I was about ready to give up all my dreams for him. He talked of whisking me off overseas, and we were going to travel the world together. I was days away from dropping out when he broke up with me. I was shattered, of course, but in retrospect... it was absolutely the right thing for me. We would have held each other back, and I never would have become a lawyer and have this kick-ass job that I seriously love if I'd followed after him."

Mom bobbed her head in agreement while I sat there playing with my food and feeling like I'd been spooning in mouthfuls of desert rocks.

"And long distance doesn't work either. I know you talked about trying that out for a while, but I dated a guy one summer a few years back. He was from New York, and we had this whirlwind affair. We were totally in love with each other and determined to make it work, but..." She tutted and shook her head. "Three months of long distance and we quickly realized it was going to be too hard to maintain. It's a serious drag, lil bro." Her smile was sad as she nudged my shoulder. "I really like Sienna. You guys were great together, and at first, I was rooting for you, but... if you didn't end it now, long distance was going to kill you guys. I'm really sorry to say this, because I know it hurts... but Zan, you did the right thing."

Hearing that from the person I respect most in this world had more impact than anything else. We'd kind of already talked about it before I broke things off, so I knew where she stood. But hearing it again at that dinner secured my resolve, and it's stopped me every time I've picked up the phone to reconnect with Sienna.

If I stay in touch, I won't be able to resist her, and we'll just get back together again only to repeat all this drama later on down the line.

It feels so wrong to not be with her.

But logically, it's the right thing to do.

I need to spread my wings, and I can't do that if she's holding on to them. And it's the same for her. I'll just hold her back. She needs to have her own dreams and figure out what she wants to do with her life. If she stayed with me, she'd rearrange her life to accommodate mine, and I don't want her missing out on cool senior-year events because she's waiting for my phone call or whatever.

Both my parents regret not breaking up, and I don't want to end up like them. I fought for Sienna and me. I fought all fucking year, but... as much as it kills me to say it... their logic has finally won me over.

"I'll never love anyone but you."

Her words haunt me, because I feel the same way. I can't imagine ever feeling for another girl what I feel for Sen. She's my Sparky... the one who ignited my soul. I love her. I love her so fucking much.

But I'm only eighteen. And I've never experienced anyone else. How do I really know what love is like if I've never felt heartache?

Is that logic completely fucked, or do I have a point here?

"Shit, I don't know," I mumble, snatching the last of

my socks out of the drawer and dumping them into my duffel bag.

I'm staying the night at Dad's place.

I'm leaving for Kelsey U tomorrow morning, and I can't wait to get there.

I just want to hit the road and get moving.

I need to start this next chapter of my life. Because staying in Everett, knowing Sienna's only a block away, is killing me.

The ache inside me is immense, and it's taking all my willpower not to run through the night and see her one more time. It's raining outside, pelting down, but I can picture myself running through those fat drops to get to her.

But she told me to go.

She screamed at me to leave.

I can't torture her by turning back up at her door.

I can't—

Something sharp hits my window, and I jerk toward the sound.

Walking over, I pull back the curtain and spot Sienna's face, rain running down her skin like tears.

"Sen?" I hurry to push up the frame. "What are you doing here?"

She sniffs, slashing rain off her cheeks and giving me a tumultuous smile. "Noah told me you'd be here tonight."

"Yeah." I swallow, drinking her in. Her shirt is saturated, sticking to her skin and showing me everything.

I miss that body.

I miss her touch.

I ache.

I pine.

"I know you're leaving tomorrow, and I'm not here to try and persuade you or win you back or anything. I just..." Her chin bunches. "I just miss... I miss..."

Before she can say anything else, I reach out through the window, wrapping my arm around her waist and pulling her inside.

CHAPTER 32
SIENNA

I cling to his shoulders, no doubt saturating him.

I didn't mean to run through the rain to reach him. But I'd been on a group call with Emily, Olivia, and Georgie... and Zander's name had come up. They didn't mean to start talking about him, but when I heard it was his final night and he'd be at his dad's house, I felt this overwhelming compulsion that I couldn't fight.

So I snuck out my back door and ran through the rain.

Because I needed to see him one more time.

Zander lets me go, holding me by the shoulders and stepping back from me. He looks worried, his beautiful face puckering into a gentle frown.

"What's the matter?" he whispers, his eyes darting to his bedroom door before landing back on me.

"I'm sorry," I mouth, then find my voice. "I'm sorry. I know I should go, but... my heart hurts so bad." I whimper, then let out this little hiccup before pushing through the rest. "I just needed to see you one more time before you left. I just want to feel your arms around me again."

He doesn't hesitate. Pulling me against him, he envelops me in a hug. Our bodies press together, and I sink into his embrace, loving him with every fiber of my being.

His breath fans against my ear as he leans his cheek against mine, then starts kissing me. Running little nibbles from my earlobe to my lips, he brings me home with his luscious tongue. I deepen the kiss, a swift urgency running through me as I can sense the clock ticking away in the back of my mind.

He's leaving soon.

Make the most of this, because it might never happen again.

We start to undress each other in a frenzy. My wet clothes slap onto his floor while we stumble, jerking our layers off and kissing with a frantic passion.

I can sense his need. It's as strong and deep as mine, and I go with it, flopping back onto his bed and pulling him on top of me.

My body is aching for him, my insides wet and pleading as I drop my legs open. He kisses me deeply, cupping the back of my head and plunging into me with one swift move. My cry is caught by his tongue. He swallows my moans of pleasure, drinking my sounds away as he thrusts into me again and again. I raise my hips to meet his and we move together, clinging and connecting with this feral urgency that I can't stop.

I need this.

He needs this too. I can feel it.

We've been starved of each other this week, and we're making up for lost time.

"I love you," I murmur against his mouth, trailing my hand down his body and squeezing his ass, propelling him deeper into my body.

He complies, plowing into me with a grunt, then whispering words of affection. "I'll always love you, Sen. My sweet Sparky."

I smile against his chin, groaning when he hits a sweet spot. He picks up his pace, his heart thundering against my chest as he loses himself in me.

Our groans mingle together, his mouth hovering against mine as his pants increase. He's going to come soon, and I'm about to remind him about protection when he whispers, "I'll pull out before I pop, okay? Or do you want me to suit up?"

I shake my head, hating the idea of a rubber sheath, needing his skin on my skin. Needing our private places to be connected with no barriers between us.

"It's okay." I kiss his chin. "I trust you."

He plunges into me again and I whimper, loving the way he fills me so completely.

Opening my eyes, I study his face. His expression buckles, his mouth popping open as he thrusts hard and deep two more times before whipping out of me and ejaculating on my stomach. He jerks and moans above me, and then I wrap my arms around him, pulling him flush against me and loving him with everything I have.

I cling to his shoulders, kissing his neck and closing my eyes. I breathe him in, absorbing all I can, needing this memory to last forever.

As we slowly float back down from our high, he peels his sweaty body off mine and hands me a wad of tissues. I clean up my stomach, wiping his cum away and fighting another round of tears. I'm going to have to leave him soon, climb out that window and walk my ass back home.

But then he pulls me close. His lips brush my shoulder as he nestles my back to his chest, spooning me against his solid body.

"You're so beautiful. I love being with you so much."

I smile into his pillow, drinking in his husky voice and trying to memorize the sound of it. "I love being with you too." I'm trying so hard not to ruin this perfect moment by lamenting that it's our last time together.

"You'll always be with me, Sen. Always." He nuzzles my neck, and I roll over to face him.

Hooking my leg over his hip, I wriggle our bodies together again. Our messy sweetness sticks to our skin, my hurried clean-up not quite getting it all. But I don't care. I want it to soak into me forever. I need this boy to always stay with me. Even just the smallest part of him.

"I'll never forget you," I promise. "And I'll always love you."

"Me too." His smile is beautiful, and I soak it in. "My first love."

My heart trills and flails, and I'm not sure how I'm going to leave him.

But I don't have to make that decision until the morning. Because our eyes drift shut together, and we cling to each other until the soft light of dawn rouses me.

I can hear movement in the hallway outside, and I'm pretty sure Zander's dad is up and about. If he catches me in here, there'll no doubt be hell to pay, so I slip out of bed.

The move wakes Zander and he sits up with a groggy frown, watching me get dressed.

I zip my fly, then pull the damp, crinkled T-shirt back over my body. His gaze is on me the whole time, and I stop, drinking him in one last time.

"Good luck, Zander. I hope all your dreams come true."

His eyes glass with tears, and I bend down and kiss him. Our lips press together, and it's like they know this is the last goodbye, because we linger for a long, thick beat before finally pulling apart.

My smile feels heavy and sad as I brush my fingers down his face, then head for the window.

"This might not be forever, Sen." His voice catches as if he's trying to comfort himself. "If we're meant to be... we'll be."

I smile at him, the thought giving me enough hope to whisper, "I know."

Climbing out the window, I run through the misty air. The morning sun is attempting to dry the rain-soaked ground, and the humidity clings to me. By the time I walk through the back door, my head is pounding and I feel like throwing up.

I'm not sure why. Maybe I'm just completely drained after days of mourning my man.

But last night was a bit of closure, I guess.

At least we're not leaving with anger sparking between us. Just deep sadness.

I think about our night together. The feel of his arms

around me and how I felt so safe and secure in his embrace.

Our frenzied lovemaking... that urgent connection we both so desperately needed.

I'll never forget the feel of him inside me.

He's a part of my soul. No matter what happens.

I reach the kitchen and find my dad sitting at the dining table. He has a mug of coffee in his hand and a look on his face that tells me he knows exactly where I've been. I take in his sad smile and suddenly burst into tears.

"Aw, Blue." Standing tall, he walks across to me, gathering me into his arms and taking a seat. Snuggling me on his lap, he rests his head against mine, letting me cry buckets into his shirt. "I know it doesn't feel like it right now, but it's all going to be okay. You're going to get through this." He kisses my forehead, rubbing my back while I whimper against him.

And then Mom appears. Tying her bathrobe at the waist, she runs over, wrapping her arms around us and holding on tight.

I draw strength from their embrace and words of comfort.

"Never regret this love, my darling. He'll always be a part of your story, and once the pain dies down... he'll be a part you can cherish and remember with a smile."

I know they're right.

Zander will always be a part of me.

I just didn't realize how much...

PRESENT DAY...

CHAPTER 33
ZANDER

If I'd known that was the last time I was ever going to see her, would I have done anything differently?

My chest hurts just thinking about it.

"Let's go play some ball at the park." Tyrell grabs a football. "I need to shake off this shit."

I'm all for that! Gotta get Sienna out of my mind before it crushes me. I always hate it when I get caught in a moment thinking about our miserable end. It was the best sex we'd ever had, and I thought I was cool with it being the last... I just hadn't known how much I'd miss her when I went away to college.

I tried to forget her. Tried to spread my wings and fly, but there were so many moments I wanted to share with her. She stayed with me, clung to my brain, my heart, my soul. And my need for her wouldn't let up no matter what I tried.

Which is why, during my three-day Christmas break, I came back for her. Screwing waiting until the end of the season. I couldn't keep going without her.

My insides start to burn, an acidic taste filling my mouth as I try not to relive the worst holiday of my life.

Shit. Don't go there, man. Just forget it. Forget her!

"Let's go, bro." Grady slaps my leg, forcing me up.

We drag Carson's ass off the couch as well, ignoring his grumbling complaints as we walk out into the sunshine and head for the closest park. It's two blocks down and isn't part of Nolan University's campus. It's a public area with a playground and water fountain. The big green field is lined with trees, and it's the perfect place to throw a ball around.

I catch it when Tyrell fires it my way, then run back two paces, launching a perfect spiral through the air. Grady sprints down the field, plucking the ball out of the air and diving around Carson, who tries to tackle him. Slamming the ball onto the ground, he lets out a loud whoop, doing a backflip, then getting pushed off his feet by Carson, who gathers the ball and starts sprinting.

Wily grabs him before he can get too far, lifting him off his feet in a quick fireman's hold before spinning him around while he yells obscenities that make us all laugh.

I share a smile with Tyrell, who rolls his eyes and starts jogging over to break up any potential fight. Carson's got a quick-fire temper that can be fucking lethal if not monitored. And Tyrell seems to know how to calm the guy down.

Wily throws the guy off his back, and Carson lands with an "Oomph" before shooting to his feet and jumping on Wily, putting him in a quick choke hold in order to wrestle the ball out of his hands. It bounces wildly, and they scramble after it while I stand there grinning and wishing football could be as untamed as what we're doing right now. There's nothing like scrapping for a ball. Coach never lets us do it for fear of injuries, but he isn't here right now.

Carson snatches the ball and starts running. He's a hell of a lot faster than Wily, and the wide receiver leaves the lineman in his dust.

"Carson!" I shout, raising my hands and trying to warn him about the bullet coming up behind him.

Grady's the fastest guy on the team, and Carson doesn't sense his approach quick enough. With a little yell, he hurls the ball my way, but the pass is made reckless by Grady's side tackle. The ball ends up arcing straight over my head and bouncing into the playground behind me.

I shake my head as the two guys start to tussle and figure Tyrell can take this one while I retrieve the ball. Running into the playground, I head for the sand pit, where a little girl with blonde ringlets is gathering up the ball.

Aw, cutie.

I crouch down with a smile, ready to get the ball back, when the air is knocked clean from my lungs. My lips part as I watch this blonde cherub totter toward me. Holy shit. She looks exactly like Monica did as a toddler. Photos of my older sister as a baby flash through my head, and I can't believe the similarities. It's freaky.

The little girl stops a few feet away from me and holds up the ball. "Bawl."

I nod and can't help grinning at her. "That's right. Football."

"Foo-bawl." Her sweet little voice pitches with excitement, and she laughs.

"Do you want to throw it to me?" I beckon with my fingers, then glance around, wondering where this little girl's parents are.

She giggles again, then throws the ball with a little grunt, raising her hands in the air with a cheer when it lands a foot away from me before dribbling to a stop by my feet.

"Good job, kid." I wink at her, then laugh when she claps her hands.

Far out. That smile is just like Monica's.

This is seriously freaking me out.

"Zan-Man, let's go!" Wily calls me, holding up his hands to catch the ball. I fire it through the air, then jog back to the edge of the field, turning one more time to look at the little girl. She's crouching down in the sand, gathering handfuls and creating a little mountain.

For reasons I can't even explain, I find myself watching her until my friends are shouting at me again.

"Dude, what's up?" Grady calls across the grass. "Let's go, brother."

"Just give me a sec!" I hold up my finger, pulling out my phone and calling my sister while this little girl is still within sight.

"'Sup, lil bro?"

"Do you have a daughter I don't know about?"

"Ew, no. Why would I ever have kids?" Her reaction makes me laugh, and I shake my head.

My sister has taken independent woman to the next level. She's in a relationship now, but who knows if it'll last. She likes to go intense and hard... for short bursts of time. That just seems to be her style. I get why she'd never want to bring kids into that equation.

"Why are you calling to ask me stupid questions? You know I'm at work, right?"

"It's Sunday."

"I have a big case."

"Oh, well, sorry. I just..." Shaking my head yet again, I gaze at the little girl and let out a breathy laugh. "You must have a doppelgänger in Nolan, sis, because I am staring at a kid who looks just like you when you were two. You know that picture on Dad's office desk?"

"The one of me playing on the beach in that frilly abomination Mom insisted on dressing me in?"

I laugh. "That's the one. Well, this little girl right here isn't in frills, but man... she looks just like you. It's freaking me out."

Monica snorts. "Well, her mother must be very beautiful, then."

"And look just like you." I start to search the playground for her, but there are so many parents around. A group of moms is standing by the sand pit, watching their kids and talking together. My eyes skim across them, but I don't see any Monica replicas. And the rest of the playground seems clear too. Darting my gaze back to the girl, I shake my head again. "It's seriously incredible."

"You're still staring at her, aren't you?"

"I can't help it."

"Yeah, well, you might want to stop in case her big bad daddy is there and wants to pound on some freaky-ass guy who's staring at his kid."

"Yeah, good point." I turn my back to the playground. "Not the pounding shit, because I can hold my own." I can practically hear her eyes rolling. "But I don't want to be putting creeper vibes out there."

"Good boy."

I grin. "Glad you didn't get knocked up without me knowing."

"I do my best. Love you, bro."

"Love you." I hang up and look over my shoulder again... in time to miss the pass coming right at me. It fires straight past my head and rolls toward the playground again.

"Seriously, Zan! Come on, man." Carson scowls at me. "Get your head in the game."

I raise my hand in apology and run back to the playground, scooping up the ball and crouching down to grin at the girl again.

She smiles back at me, her little nose wrinkling in a way that's all too familiar.

My stomach hitches.

"Zoey!" a woman calls, and the girl turns, her blonde curls bobbing as she waves.

"Mommy!"

"Hey, baby girl! Time to go!" Her mother's voice brightens as she bustles over, pushing a stroller and hitching a bag on her shoulder. Quickly sending a text, she puts the phone away and then glances across at her daughter, freezing when she notices me.

Holy shit.

My lips part, my heart catapulting into my throat as I

jolt to my feet and gape at a gorgeous blonde with bright blue eyes.

She gapes right back at me, and then my world starts to splinter when the little girl yells, "Mommy!" again and runs over to her.

Mommy?

Fuck no.

What?

My ears start ringing as I watch the girl I fell in love with in high school scoop her daughter into her arms. She can't take her eyes off me, and I wish I had something intelligent to say, but all I can whisper is "Sparks."

She shakes her head, clutching her daughter and choking out, "Nope!" before snatching the stroller handle and running out of the playground like she's just seen a ghost.

Zander and Sienna's second-chance romance continues in THE FOREVER PLAY.

Available on Amazon in April 2025.

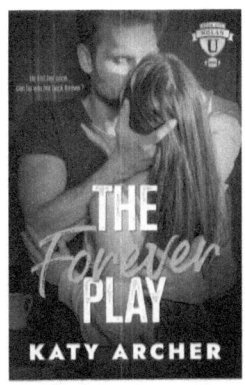

NOTE FROM KATY

Dear reader,

Thank you so much for jumping into the Nolan U Football series with me. I really hope you enjoyed Zander and Sienna's first-love story. There's something so incredibly powerful about first romances. There's a sweetness and purity to them. An innocence. And it was such a privilege capturing all of that with Zander and Sienna. I love their first kiss, their first time...the intensity of their feelings for each other. And I can't wait to see them reunited in THE FOREVER PLAY.

I'm a huge fan of second-chance romance and theirs is going to be a doozy! They have a lot to work through and so many secrets from the past will be unearthed as they find their way back to each other. Get ready for emotional arguments, passionate kisses and adorable daddy-daughter moments that will melt your heart. Big football players and an precocious two-year-old? It doesn't get cuter than that.

I seriously cannot wait!

If you enjoyed *The First Play*, I would so appreciate you leaving an honest review on Amazon and/or Goodreads. Even just a star rating is helpful. You don't have to write anything if you don't want to. But star ratings and even short reviews really help validate the book, letting readers know it's worth a shot. It also tells Amazon and Goodreads that this book is worth shining a spotlight on. I know there are a bunch of readers out there who love college sports romance just as much as we do. If you can help me reach them, then that would be freaking fantastic.

Thanks for the assist!

I'd also like to thank a few key people who have been instrumental in helping me get this book off the ground —Megan, Kristin, Beth and Rachael. Working with you guys is seriously the best. I love all our interactions. You are talented, amazing women who I really admire.

Maggie and Trudi—what would I do without you guys? You make everything better and I love every one of our conversations. You uplift me in a way no one else can.

My review team—wow! You guys! I love you all. Thank you for every kind word, every graphic, every beautiful message about my books. I seriously couldn't do this without you and I'm so grateful for your time and support.

My readers—I couldn't do this without you either. Thank you a million times over. Thank you for loving this Nolan U world and making my job so incredibly enjoyable.

My family—thanks for giving me a life of adventure. I've seen so much of the world and experienced so many incredible things from the time I was a baby. I'm still traveling the world as much as I can and it's all because of you.

My first love—thank you for a love beyond compare. It's unrelenting, unconditional and something I can always rely on. I love you now and forever.

xoxo
Katy

ALSO BY KATY ARCHER

NOLAN U HOCKEY

Hockey House V-cards (prequel)

The Forbidden Freshman

The Heart Stealer

The Game Changer

The Love Penalty

The Only Goal

The Forever Game

NOLAN U FOOTBALL

Releasing in 2025

The First Play (prequel)

The Forever Play

The Off-Limits Play

The Surprise Play

The Illicit Play

The Perfect Play

The Christmas Play

NOLAN U BASKETBALL

Releasing in 2026

In development

CONTACT KATY

I love to hear from my readers, so feel free to email me anytime. You can also find out more on my website.

EMAIL: katy@katyarcher.com

WEBSITE: www.katyarcher.com

And if you want to connect with me on social and see pretty reels and teasers from the books, you can find me Addicted to College Sports Romance on...

INSTAGRAM
@addictedtocollegesportsromance

FACEBOOK
@collegesportsromancebooks

TIKTOK
@katyarcherbooks

www.ingramcontent.com/pod-product-compliance
Lightning Source LLC
Chambersburg PA
CBHW031705170626
46808CB00005B/1619